ഇ Taelo Character Stories ര

Ron Mueller

ஒ Taelo Character Stories ଷ

By: *Ron Mueller*

Around the World Publishing, LLC
Cincinnati, Ohio

This story is a work of fiction. Names, characters, places, and incidents either are products of the author's imagination or are used fictitiously. Any resemblance to actual events or locales or persons, living or dead, is entirely coincidental.

Taelo Character Stories©

ISBN 13: 978-1-68223-842-4

Distributed by Ingram
Eagle by: © Teekaygee @Dreamstime
Cover Design By: Ron Mueller

The Stories of Taelo are set in the distant past, long before the time currently given as to when people migrated into the western hemisphere.

This is purposely done since the stories are meant to engage the reader in a story and not relate exact history.

The adventures of Taelo and Golden Hawk, sons of White Swan and Quiet Pheasant, provide the backdrop for stories featuring the values of treating others as you wish to be treated, of responsibility, integrity, honesty, contribution, and the joy of learning.

Books by Ron Mueller
Fiction Series
The Taelo Series
The Early Years
The Golden Feather
Journey of Discovery
Dangerous Passage
Condor Clan Slingers
Circumvention
The Journey of Sages
Future Leaders Journey
Taelo Collection

A Taelo Story
White Swan and Quiet Pheasant
The Child's Name
Floating Cloud
Quiet Rabbit
Busy Bee
Little Otter & Talking Wren
Broken Spear
Burley Bear & Meadow Flower
Taelo Story Collection

The Alex Evercrest Series
The River Front
The Girl on The Grill
Missing
Maggot
Racist
Votive Candles
Windy City
Country Road
Pool of Blood
Sins of the Daughter
Body Parts
The Skull Collector
The Vanishing
The Shadow Fighter
Moonshine
Grief's Trajectory
The Magic Touch
Northern Lights
Alex Evercrest Heroine
Alex Evercrest Collection Two
New Direction
A Family Affair
Disruption
The St. Lebuinnus Church Murder

A Brian O'Neil Novel
Hawaiian Phoenix
Moon Curser
Death Broker

The Problem Solver Series
Solutions
Drug Lords
Border Crosser
The Problem Solver Collection

Science Fiction
The Savitar Series:
Journey's End
Savitar
Confluence
Savitar Series Collection

Bram Nielson Series
The Fold
The Message
Fold Wormhole
Negative Fold
Ripples in Time
Bram Nielson Collection

Single Science Fiction Books:
Current Past and Future
The Event
The Door
Viajante 7

https://www.remwriter95.net/

Dedicated to my Children

<u>Table of Content</u>

Taelo Character Stories

The Child's Name

The cool morning air refreshed White Swan as she stepped out of the warmth of her lodge. She along with all the members of the seven sub clans that made up the Elk Clan were camped in this mountain valley by the lake for their annual autumn gathering.

The clans had met here for as long as she could remember but she had listened to the stories of another valley farther to the north where the Elk Clan had first been established. And even more stories about the clan's ancestors coming to a new world across an ice bridge to the north.

She had loved sitting and listening to these stories about these ancestors who had left their land and traveled to a new one. They inspired her and they encouraged her in her pursuit of making a difference for her clan.

White Swan had only fond memories of this long oval valley, surrounded by snow-capped mountains on both sides of a long placid kidney shaped lake where she remembered running and playing as a young girl.

It was where she flirted with the young men in the other sub-clans when she was becoming a young woman.   And it was where she had met Grey Fox Running of the Elk Hide Clan.   Now she was his mate.

The sun, just breaking over the distant snowcapped mountains, made it appear as if the weeping willows and the cattails on the opposite side of the lake were growing both up into the sky and down into the dark blue lake.

The few grey, pink clouds in the sky were floating above and were also down in the lake.

White Swan admired the panoramic view of the lake framed on its edge by yellowish green willows with a few remaining leaves and a few large round granite boulders all contrasted by the backdrop of the tall lodge pole, darker green pine trees with their thin dark brown flaky bark standing ram rod straight as far as the eye could see.

Suddenly the sound of her totem, a white trumpeter swan broke the morning silence as it crested the hill and flashed white up in the morning sky.

White Swan watched in silence as the brilliant white swan flew down into the valley and the length of the lake and came to a gliding, skimming smooth landing in front of where she stood.

It then let out another quieter trumpet and floated over to rest near the large boulder and willow trees on the opposite side of the lake. Its black beak and bowed white head gave it a grace that White Swan had over the years tried to emulate.

White Swan took the arrival of her totem on the naming day to be something special.

Just then her sister, Quiet Pheasant, joined her.

Together they walked towards the lake to get a closer look at the swan.

They were up early this morning because it was the naming day and they each had a son that would select their names this day.

White Swan realized they had both recovered well from giving birth. She smiled at the thought.

They both had long black hair down to the middle of their backs and were slender and lithe. They were the same height and stood a good head shorter than a spear. Their smooth skin was the color of the autumn grass.

The distinguishing difference between them was the color of their eyes. Quiet Pheasants eyes were walnut brown almost black in color where her own eyes were more golden like a dark honey.

White Swan thought about all the mutual experiences she and Quiet Pheasant shared growing up together in the Elk Horn Clan. They were not only sisters but very close friends. They did almost everything together. This was evident when they met and mated two handsome young ambitious and successful hunters of the Elk Hide Clan.

Their relationships had flourished at the same rate and they had accepted the proposals of these two hunters on the same day.

White Swan thought about the wonderful and sad day when they both moved into the Elk Hide Clan with their mates but left their parents and friends behind.

They had each other and they were quickly accepted into and made friends with their new clan members.

White Swan could not believe the day she went to tell Quite Pheasant the good news and discovered they both had the same news.

They were pregnant!

Then a few months later, on a day very similar this one, the naming day, Quiet Pheasant gave birth to a beautiful baby boy early in the morning and White Swan heard the cry of her son at the peak of the sun's journey across the sky.

The cousin's born on the same day!

White Swan was very conscious of the close relationship the two shared and of the confidence and power they gave each other.

Today was the special day, both of their sons would be placed onto the naming hide to select the object that would determine their name.

****

Far to the north the sun was shining down on the jaggedly scarred face of the Broken Spear the Seer in the Clan of Others. He had a notch missing form his left ear and a scar from the back of his head that met the maze of scars on his face.

The sun caused sweat to bead on his forehead and then to slowly run into the corner of his closed eyes.

He had been one of the best hunters in the Clan of the Others. He had been a hunter known as Long Spear until he had defended his hunting team against the attack of a giant brown bear with a notch missing from her left ear.

She had broken his spear, bitten his face, crushed his legs and left him broken and near death.

He had successfully protected his hunting team but had paid a dear price.

His mate nursed him back to life, but it was to be a very changed life.

His new name was Broken Spear. He could no longer hunt but now he talked with the ancestors and often he could see through the eyes of the animals. He had been broken but he had been given a new gift.

At the moment he was now in the mind of an eagle. The Ancestors had summoned him to fly with this eagle so he could see a future leader that would come to the aid of his clan.

In his mind, through the sharp eyes of a white-headed eagle with a spear wide wingspan, the Seer saw the golden wavering sunlight, streaming through the broken clouds, as the morning rays lightly kissed the dark blue placid waters of the oblong lake in the center of a long oval valley surrounded by the foothills of the distant snow peaked mountains.

The Broken Spear estimated the lake to be a hefty spear's throw wide and at least twenty spear throws long. Cattail plants with their stems turned a pale tan with dried leaves and topped with reddish brown sausage like seed pods bordered its banks.

A mix of willows of all sizes completed the border of the lake. He could make out several large grey granite boulders that could serve as sitting or diving spots.

A lone white swan floated near a stand of yellowing cattails.

The eagle was riding the up draft as the air warmed by the early morning sun rose from the valley rim. The eagle was determined to only focus on one thing, whereas the Seer wanted to see all. He tried to control where the eagle looked but the eagle fought to keep its eyes on its one target.

The will of the eagle was very strong. The seer knew something special was about to happen, but he did not know what it would be.

****

The naming ceremony had started. White Swan, with her young child sitting in the seat formed by her crossed legs, sat quietly, and leaned against Grey Fox Running. Next to her was Quiet Pheasant, sitting in the same way with her child and leaning against Red Oak.

Her cheek on Grey Fox Running's shoulder, White Swan felt a warmth pass into her that was the feeling of contentment and peace.

She knew that her sister shared the same close bond with her mate.

White Swan wished her sister the same warm feeling that she had now.

White Swan was pleased that the children of all the births that had taken place thirty moon cycles ago had survived and were present for the naming ceremony.

The length of time before a name was given to a child had been decided long ago by the council of elders. It was believed that a child with a name carried the burdens of this world into land of the ancestors.

A child without a name carried no burdens and would be raised by the ancestors.

In past cycles, many children went to the ancestors with no burdens but not this time.

White Swan looked at the naming hide and the objects around its edges. Each child would be placed on the naming hide and each would select an object. This object and the child's past behaviors and actions would guide the elders and parents in selecting a final name.

White Swan looked around at the twelve children who would be selecting their object from the edge of the naming hide. The child with the most moon and sun cycles was first.

White Swan relaxed and prepared to watch each of the children.

Her son was number twelve. She would be last to hand her son to the elder sitting in the center of the naming hide.

White Swan felt the presence and heard the quite talking and watched the movement of the members of the seven sub-clans that made up the Elk clan.

They were sitting attentively all around the outside of the circle of the proud parents of the twelve to be named. The clan participation and encouragement of the young ones making the selection was part of the ceremony.

The volume and participation of the clan members was triggered by an indecisive child. This would give fuel to friends to shout out what the child should select.

The gathering seemed to relish the indecisive child.

All morning the eagle circled the valley.

The sun was almost at its zenith when White Swan looked up and seemed to look directly into the piercing yellow eyes that seemed focused on her. She imagined feeling the edge of the sharp orange beak capable of effortlessly ripping through the hide of an elk.

The eagle's white head feathers ended at the leading edge of its wings and the feathers at the ends of its spear length black wings were spread like the fingers of an open hand and were wavering as the air currents passed by them.

Its yellow claws were closed and tucked below the broad white tail that deftly guided its easy floating glide. She made note of the eagles very large size and absorbed its flowing splendor, acknowledged its dominance of the air, and then turned her attention back to the ceremony.

She had been distracted but quickly refocused when she realized that Quiet Pheasant and Red Oak were standing up to hand their young one to the elder.

He who would show the child each object spaced around the reddish-brown fox fur that was the trim around a two-spear diameter circular tan brushed elk hide.

For the eleventh time White Swan examined all the rocks of various colors, leaves, pieces of wood, bones, scraps of hide from numerous animals, feathers and feet of birds that would be waved back and forth three times in front of the child and then placed on the fox fur trim of the naming hide.

Some articles were colorfully decorated. Some were plain. Each had a meaning and would influence the name given to the child.

White Swan noted that most of the young chose the colorful objects. Long ago on this same naming hide she had chosen the white feather of the trumpeter swan.

Quiet Pheasant had chosen the feather of a pheasant. Quiet Pheasant, like Grey Fox Running had earned a second part to their names because of the observations made by their parents or the elders.

White Swan smiled as she thought about the many times her mother had threatened to add a second name for her and call her Stubborn Swan. She was the person her mother knew to be determined and stubborn but known to all only as White Swan.

White Swan released an involuntary whispering *"yes"* of approval as Quiet Pheasant's young one picked the feather of the golden hawk.

It was a symbol of bravery and leadership.

Black hair, tall and slender for his age and eyes like his mother the young boy held his feather high as he walked back toward his parents.   He would have a distinctive name.   Good choice, young *Golden Hawk,* White Swan thought as she stood up to give him and Quiet Pheasant a hug.

Quiet Pheasant's beaming face warmed White Swan's heart.

White Swan stood and her young one toddled over to his best friend and touched the feather.

White Swan noted that the two boys looked much the same. Her son was just a little taller with eyes very much like hers but with a distinct almost black edge around dark honey brown eyes. Both boys would be as tall as their fathers.

Grey Fox Running was congratulating his best friend Red Oak as White Swan gave her sister a hug.

It was her son's turn.

White Swan took note that he had been born and was now picking his name when the sun was at its zenith.

He was last and it was clear the elder was tired and he seemed relieved that the naming ceremony was coming to the end. He took the last child and began to show him all the objects before placing him in the center of the naming circle.

White Swan and Grey Fox Running watched as their son was slowly turned and shown all the articles. The elder then placed him in the center of the hide and stepped out of the circle.

The loud noise arising from the lake caused all to turn and look to where White Swan's totem was flapping its wings on the water and repeatedly trumpeting.

The eagle's piercing gaze turned to seek its goal and found what it had been patiently waiting for. Letting out an ear-splitting scream, the eagle folded his wings and shot like an a spear down, down ever so swiftly down, toward its target.

****

At the same moment but far to the North the sweat caused Broken Spear's eyes to burn, and his pulsing scars were now dark red or purple and as hard as he tried to see the boy, all he could see through the eyes of the eagle was the claw of an eagle.

He did not understand.

He was confused and frustrated.

He needed to see the boy, but the eagle's eyes were glued to its prize.

****

Instinct caused White Swan to turn her gaze from the lake back to where her son was standing. She froze in terrified fear as she watched the eagle's spear like descent toward her son who was standing in the center of the naming hide with an eagle's claw held high to the sky.

The boy and eagle clearly saw each other and nothing else.

The clan members were once again distracted as the white swan on the lake began a running wing flapping dance as it ran across the surface of the water and finally rose smoothly into the air and began a slow graceful flight around the valley.

White Swan did not look out to the lake but instinctively moved to save her son as the eagle swooped swiftly down and miraculously plucked the claw from the small up stretched hand.

Firmly clasping its prize in its claws and letting out another much closer ear-piercing cry, it opened its wings and rose swiftly upwards toward the clouds in the sky.

The boy had chosen the eagle's claw and the eagle had accepted it and by its action had chosen the boy.

The clan members turned their eyes back from the lake in time to see the exchange and then watched as the eagle rose into the sky with its prize. The white swan of equal wingspan and size gracefully followed as the eagle flew out of the valley.

For the first time during the ceremony there was silence. Nothing like this had ever happened before.

****

Far away the Seer shook his head as the vision from the mind of the eagle ended.

He had tried to see the boy.

The eagle had focused only on the claw.

The ancestors had foretold that this young one chosen by the eagle would someday save his clan.

But where was this young boy and who was he and when would the clan need saving?

The Seer knew he would have to wait for the next vision, message from the ancestors or for time to pass.

****

Tears of joy ran down White Swan's cheeks into the lightly pine scented hair of her son as she hugged him to her bosom.   She had feared the eagle would either take her son or hurt him.

The opening of the eagle's wings had totally hidden her son and for a moment total fear had overtaken her.   Then she watched the eagle take the claw from the small hand.   The eagles cry seemed to say thank you.

The strong arms of Grey Fox Running encircled them both and completed the union of the three as they knelt in the middle of the naming hide.

Golden Hawk squeezed in to give his best friend a hug and Quiet Pheasant and Red Oak all joined in, as together the two couples knelt in the center of the naming hide.

White Swan, tears of joy streaming down her cheek, thought about the choice of the claw of the eagle.   She knew it represented leadership, power, skill, and bravery.

She wondered what else it foretold.

Normally there was a waiting period until the child's name was picked but in this case the eagle had determined the name.   Her son was the claw of the eagle or *Taelo* in the language of the clan.

She stood up, held her son up and proudly introduced him as *Taelo* (Tā low) to all the clan members and Quiet Pheasant stood, held her son up and introduced *Golden Hawk.*

This was a first for the clan and it foretold of many firsts that Taelo and Golden Hawk would deliver to the clan.

And so, thousands of years ago the adventures of Taelo and Golden Hawk began.

The End

15

<u>*White Swan and Quiet Pheasant*</u>

*T*he Elk Clan had traveled to a new world. It had endured a rigorous journey across dangerous glaciers, ice cold waters, mountains, and ferocious bears. They had established themselves in a new world. Through hard work they flourished.

They had constantly been pushed south by the brutal winters and had subdivided into multiple sub-clans. There were seven "Elk" clans. White Swan was a member of the Elk Horn Clan. Its traditional leaders treated the women as their property. This was something that White Swan and her sister Quiet Pheasant railed against.

The clan's prosperity meant that there was no reason to question the culture it practiced.

White Swan, stubborn and hardheaded, struggled accepting her role in a world ruled by the men that surrounded her.

She looked into the placid water at the reflection of her sister Quiet Pheasant. She recognized her younger sister as a person with a similar attitude and with a quiet conviction as strong as hers that they would not bend to such a situation. Her sister was the one that listened deeply and then later shared her insights.

The two were just twelve moons apart in age. They would spend endless amounts of time discussing how they could influence the decisions of their parents, their parent's friends, and their own constituency. They were determined to change their society.

White Swan's eyes lifted and took in the white capped mountains with their peaks lifting high above the broken layer of white clouds.

The sun was bright, and its warming rays warmed the back of her neck as she stayed kneeling at the water's edge.

Clear, early mornings such as this were rare.

White Swan turned her eyes once again to her sister and admired her slender figure. They were very much the same.

Winter had been hard but the two had proved to be good hunters of small game. They had rebelled against staying in the camp as the other young women did. They had consistently brought in enough small game that the family always had a solid evening meal.

Their parents accepted their wandering ways and gave them the freedom to do so. Both of them knew that their daughters were not to be contained.

White Swan endured the bullying taunts of the younger men and quite openly returned the taunts by noting the weakness of those teasing her.

She ignored the stern looks from both the older men and women.

She was constantly on the lookout for ways to respond in unexpected ways.

The most troubling was when White Swan overheard one of the elders speaking to her father about doing a better job at controlling his daughters. Quiet Pheasant overheard the same warning. The two discussed this and what they might do to maintain their freedom to do what they wanted to do.

There seemed to be no direct way.

They came up with an approach that would serve them well throughout their lifetime. They began with their parents, prepared a celebration dinner, and let them know what great parents they were.

Their mother pulled them aside and asked what they were up to.

White Swan replied that they were only treating everyone the way they wished to be treated.

Quiet Pheasant's assurance made their mother smile.

"I will help the two of you," their mother said with a smile. She too knew the frustration of fitting into the hard work of the camp while the young men went off on their hunting adventures.

The change in their behavior at first yielded a positive response but several of the older members of the leadership team continued to rail against the fact that the two were not engaged in the same manner as the other young women.

White Swan and Quiet Pheasant continued their excursions out into the wilderness. They roamed the hills like the tomboys they were.

Their father taught them how to hunt and how to protect themselves. He was very proud of his daughters capabilities.

He showed them not only how to protect themselves from the wild animals with spears and a small stone hammer, but also from other humans.

White Swan listened to her father as he showed her how to use the power of a larger opponent to overcome him. This was an ancient art that had been passed down to him from his father and grandfather.

The direct support of their father was important to both she and Quiet Pheasant.

Quiet Pheasant commented later that their father was worried about what some of the elders might do because they were breaking the unwritten rules of the clan.

Everyday White Swan and Quiet Pheasant would go out to a secluded location and practice what their father had taught them. It was not long before White Swan was certain that she and Quiet Pheasant could beat any of the young men in a one-on-one fight.

They did their victory dance in celebration of the praise they received from both their father and mother.

They continued to practice their self-defense and they continued to hunt.

They were now on a hunt and were now on the attack.

White Swan felt the early morning sun on her neck. Her breathing was deep and steady. Her heartbeat was a deep steady rhythm. Her legs were taking long smooth strides. Her feet barely touched the ground. She felt the pure energy rise into her mind. She knew she was in the other world where she could do anything and be anyone.

Her eyes were glued to the body of the large woolly buffalo racing at top speed. She was running at its side. She kept the young bull running away from the herd.

She was slowly moving him farther away and up toward the thick pine covered hills that surrounded the long flat valley.

The sky above was a clear blue, the wind was in her face. It was a glorious day.

Out to her left she looked at her sister. Quiet Pheasant carried a spear in each hand and her arms pumped back and forth as if she was using them to power her swiftly moving legs. Her feet seemed to barely touch the ground as she fluidly kept pace with the swiftly moving young buffalo that she had selected for herself.

They were duplicate images. Boths racing next to young buffaloes that were headed toward the forest.

White Swan smiled and turned her attention back to her buffalo. She was confident they both would be taking the humps of these young bulls as rewards to their mother.

Her long black hair flew parallel to the ground as she picked up the pace. It was almost time to bring down the young bull. White Swan judged the distance to the edge of the woods. She would put down her bull at the base of the tree that she would use to hang him up in.

Guide my hands she thought up to the ancestors of old. She then raced out ahead of the young bull. She had carried the spear in her right hand with the head pointed behind her. This was the way the old hunter had said it should be done. Once she was ahead of the bull, she planted the butt of the spear in the ground and simultaneously placed the head just inside of the bulls left front leg.

The bull ran up onto the spear and slid on his knees as his heart stopped.

She stopped. She glanced to her left where she made eye contact with Quiet Pheasant who had done the same and was looking to her right.

Both were prepared to use their other spear should it be necessary. It was not. Their first spears went almost halfway into the young bull's chest. Their front legs had buckled. They had died instantly and appeared to be bowing to the tree that stood only a body length away.

White Swan again looked at Quiet Pheasant. Simultaneously they both let out their adrenalin powered cries of victory and raced toward each other and did a whooping dance. They had talked about this moment for most of the winter months. They had practiced running full speed carrying their spears. They had asked about hunting buffalo and listened to all the old warriors as they explained how to hunt buffalo.

Only their father had described the technique they had just used.

"Only the fastest hunters and only those with enough stamina to run their buffalo long and hard can hunt the buffalo and never throw their spear. They do not need strength.

They need speed and stamina.

Both of you can do it," he had explained with a twinkle in his eye.

He knew what White Swan and Quiet Pheasant wanted. He wished he could be with them to witness their success.

White Swan had thanked him and after a few more question, she and Quiet Pheasant had started their preparations.

Their preparation had been rewarded.

"One for each of us. Now the hard work begins. We need to get them off the ground where the wolves and bears cannot get to them. Let's go get our gear and get them skinned and the meat into the trees," White Swan said once the two of them had recovered from the run and the excitement of the kill.

"You know that now the elders will really be upset about our behavior," Quiet Pheasant commented.

"Oh, this will raise many questions and will surely get us into trouble. How could two weak women dare to hunt the buffalo," White Swan responded in a deep voice and then she let out a laugh and enjoyed the fact that Quiet Pheasant was laughing with her.

"Yes, father will have his hands full dealing with the elders, but he will be laughing with us, and mother will help by cooking a dinner for all the elders," Quiet Pheasant added.

White Swan and Quiet Pheasant managed to get the buffalo skinned and the majority of the meat hung up into the high branches of the tree. They moved all the scraps away from where they had hauled the meat into the high branches.

They harnessed themselves to the travois loaded with the two shoulder humps, two hides, the tongues, hearts, livers, and kidneys of the young buffaloes.

They would return to the camp well after dark. Their load was all they could handle. It was much harder than they had imagined it would be.

"Well, I was worried that my two daughters had met their fate," their father spoke up as he met them about halfway back to camp. He took in contents of the travois.

"Oh, this will be so much fun. My two daughters have just passed the challenge of becoming hunters and young warriors.

This after I agreed to make sure you behaved as appropriate for young women of the clan," he continued as he gave them both a hug.

"I will pull the travois into camp. You two go to the river and clean up. I am sure your mother will have some of the hump meat prepared by the time you get done," their father directed as they came within sight of their lodge.

His pulling in a travois loaded with some hides would seem normal. He had decided that confronting the issue the next day would make it easier.

White Swan was surprised by her father's enthusiastic headlong attack on the customs of the clan. He insisted that she and Quiet Pheasant be recognized as warriors and hunters of the clan.

To her amazement the elders yielded to giving them the title of hunters but would not yield to giving them the distinction of being warriors.

The autumn clan meeting was fast approaching. The clan meetings were a time of celebration and of romance.

White Swan had her eyes on a specific young warrior and hunter in the Elk Hide Clan named Grey Fox Running.

She mentioned this to Quiet Pheasant who replied that his buddy, Red Oak was of interest to her.

"We need to get them out alone and see what they are made of. I do not want to be a servant or maid to any man," White Swan commented.

"Let's take them on a hunt and see how they react when we out hunt them," Quiet Pheasant suggested.

In the sun cycles leading up to their departure for the Elk Clan gathering, White Swan put all of her talent to work.

She would give her mate to be, gifts he would be proud to wear. She made a vest and a pair of footwear. She was not sure of the foot size and left them partially undone so she could custom fit them.

Quiet Pheasant followed her lead and did the same. Their vests were similar, but the fur trim and the front fastenings were unique in each case.

White Swan used the toenails from a dire wolf that went through an opposing leather loop whereas Quiet Pheasant used hand carved pieces of red oak wood that went through slits on the opposing side of the vest.

White Swan used grey fox fur for her trim, while Quiet Pheasant used red fox fur for the trim. The smooth, soft finish of the leather, the minimal but distinctive trim, the rabbit fur lining on the inside all combined to make the gifts unique and valuable.

They both wanted to display their skill at providing clothing and they planned to later show off their cooking skills.

"I see you have your eyes set on some young men," their mother commented when she saw what White Swan and Quiet Pheasant were doing.

"Make sure of the character of the man, do not go only on his looks," was her only comment.

"Is it OK if he is also good looking," White Swan said with a chuckle?

She got a nod and a smile from her mother.

Two sun cycles later the Elk Horn Clan departed for the Clan gathering. The clan was hoping to be the first to arrive. A few sun cycles later the valley came into sight.

White Swan and Quiet Pheasant pulled their travois as the Elk Horn Clan crested the hill.

The oblong valley bordered by the thick stand of brown trunked, dark green pine, stretched out before them. At the far end the crystal-clear waters of a lake reflected the blue of the sky and the yellow of the weeping willow trees that graced its banks. The thick grasses and drying flower stems undulated, as the wind at their back passed the clan and seemed to massage the tall thick mass of grass that spread before them.

They were the first clan to arrive. They would have the choice of sites. White Swan let out a sigh of relief. The burden of carrying water would be easier. She looked over at Quiet Pheasant and they both gave a knowing smile.

All the sub clans of the Elk Clan camped on one side of the lake. Every season one clan stayed behind to ensure the valley was put back to its natural state. The stones for the fire pits and the stones used to hold down the lodge hides were gathered and put in small separate piles.

White Swan and Quiet Pheasant put all their effort into getting their campsite established. They gathered and positioned the rocks for the fire pit. They placed the stones around the base of their family lodge.

They put out the boundary markers.

Once their camp was complete, they disappeared to scout out the valley, the forest, and the other side of the low mountains.

They traveled a path they knew well in a steady jog. The two knew every trail, every major outcropping, and every bend. In the past, they had been to the head of the stream feeding the lake. This valley was theirs. They knew every major feature.

Periodically they would launch their small spears and a rabbit would meet its end. These they prepared for their lunch or dinner. White Swan had let her parents know that they would be back late or in the morning. Their goal was to scout out the game on the other side of the mountains. They were looking for buffalo.

They needed to test out the young men they had set their eyes on and had decided to take them on a hunt.

A few days later Quiet Pheasant tapped White Swan on the shoulder and pointed to the arriving clan. The Elk Hide Clan leader carried his spear with its distinctive red leather piece of Elk Hide high in the air as the clan entered camp.

White Swan listened to the song being chanted and sung by the on-coming clan.

"I will need to change that if I ever go into that clan," she quietly said to Quiet Pheasant.

"I agree but our quests seem to be enjoying their part in singing it," Quiet Pheasant replied.

White Swan and Quiet Pheasant walked by as the Elk Hide Clan organized their camp site. There were many young women coming of age. Competition for their young men was going to be high. White Swan had decided they would make immediate contact with their two young warriors.

White Swan's and Quiet Pheasant had gentle totem, but they were fierce competitors, and they were non-traditional. Let the beauties of the clan wait for their suitors to come to them. White Swan was going to capture hers while the others waited.

White Swan waited until the two were walking toward the upstream crossing where the small river fed the lake. She then approached them. Quiet Pheasant was at her side.

After some small talk and greetings, White Swan suggested they go and hunt a buffalo together.

The unusual suggestion stopped the conversation in its tracks.

She let the silence hang and returned a steady gaze back at the surprised Grey Fox Running.

Quiet Pheasant was doing the same with Red Oak.

The two young men looked at each other and with a nod they seemed to agree, and both smiled and accepted the invitation with the simple question, When?

White Swan suggested they leave early the next morning. They would meet at the spot they were on, just before sunrise.

She and Quiet Pheasant turned and walked back to their camp and shared the news with their parents.

"Don't scare those two young men," their mother commented when she learned of the upcoming hunt.

"Yes, I am getting too old to hunt for two mate-less women," their father commented as he chuckled.

"We will know by tomorrow night whether you have two mate-less daughters or two handsome new members of our family," White Swan replied.

That evening she and Quiet Pheasant danced the same victory dance they had done when they killed their first buffalo.

Now they would see if they could get a mate by sundown the following day.

Once White Swan and Quiet Pheasant had departed, Red Oak and Grey Fox Running were left standing looking at the two beauties that were walking away. They were somewhat disoriented.

"Did we just agree to go buffalo hunting with two very good-looking women," Red Oak commented as he shook his head?

All he could remember was gazing into the depth of Quiet Pheasant's dark black eyes.

"Yes, we leave before sunrise in the morning. Let's go get ready. I am not sure how we will hunt together. This should be one of the more interesting hunts we go on. I am not sure what or who is hunting or being hunted," Grey Fox Running replied as he remembered the honey-colored eyes that had penetrated his soul.

Grey Fox Running spent the rest of the evening replaying the encounter he had experienced with White Swan.

The next morning White Swan and Quiet Pheasant were waiting for Grey Fox Running and Red Oak. After a quick good morning White Swan led the group on a steady jogging pace along the almost invisible trail across the mountain.

The grey of early morning, the mist hanging low against the mountain and the quiet of the thick forest of leafless maples and dark green pine encouraged and enriched the quiet the four were sharing.

The sun slowly dispersed the mist and began to warm the air. The awakening of the morning seemed to draw out the low melodic chant she and Quiet Pheasant always shared as they jogged.

They harmonized and when one took the pitch up the other would go in the opposite direction. Soon all four were harmonizing together.

White Swan listened and smiled as Grey Fox Running and Red Oak took up the chant. They added depth and resonance.

She thought that the four sounded good together.

Then ahead the sea of bison lay before them. White Swan did not at first see them. They seemed to be the brown floor at the bottom of the mountain. Then her mind interpreted the scene, and she realized the herd went out as far as the eye could see into the dark blue cloudless horizon beyond.

She thanked the Ancients for providing the buffalo.

She stopped at the edge of the forest. The buffalo herd was no more than a few hundred feet away.

"Let's talk about how we will get our buffalo. We will only kill one. Quiet Pheasant and I will select a young bull, bring him to you, and drop him at your feet. If we miss you will get your turn. If we are successful you will do the skinning and prepare a travois to carry it back to the valley," White Swan said quietly.

"Why only one," both Red Oak and Grey Fox Running asked?

"Because we will need to carry everything we kill back across the mountain to the valley," Quiet Pheasant replied.

White Swan watched as the two men looked at each other.

"What more could we ask for than to have the buffalo delivered to us at our feet," Red Oak replied with a smile.

"Those two seem to have the guidance of the ancestors. They move so smoothly and effortlessly," Grey Fox Running commented as he watched White Swan point to the buffalo she had picked out.

The two exchanged comments about the ease and relaxed way the two young women were working together.

Red Oak wondered whether they be would strong enough to drive their spears into the bull for the kill?

White Swan took the side closest to the herd and Quite Pheasant paralleled her on the outside. Together, slowly with an ease that defied the situation they eased the young bull away from the edge of the herd and had it moving in an almost straight line toward where Grey Fox Running and Red Oak stood silently watching.

White Swan vocalized a sharp yell and was immediately joined by Quite Pheasant as the Bull began to run.

It was then that both Grey Fox Running and Red Oak noticed the inner spears each young woman carried was pointed backwards while the outer spears were pointed forward.

Both voiced the question of how they would be able to spear the bull?

The bull was quickly approaching the two young men when to their amazement both of the women increased their speed to run in front of the bull.

White Swan let out a loud, "Now" as she stepped ever so slightly in and planted the butt of the spear into the ground and placed the tip just inside the front leg of the bull.

Quite Pheasant did the right-hand opposite.

The two spears instantly killed the young bull who came to his knees less than a spears length from Grey Fox Running and Red Oak.

White Swan and Quite Pheasant let out their victory cry and did their round dance. Then they both turned to the two thoroughly amazed young men and in an exaggerated show, pointed to the bull.

"Will you teach us how to hunt like this," the two men asked in unison.

"We will only teach our mates," White Swan replied in a bold way.

She was, in fact, immediately afraid of the reply.

"I don't know what to say. They hunt well, but can they cook, and will they be able to wash off the smell of the sweat mixed with the blood of the buffalo? What do you think," Grey Fox Running replied as he turned to Red Oak?

"I think that we are out classed, out hunted and should concentrate on getting this buffalo skinned. I did notice a small spring back in the woods that will provide both water to drink and to wash off," Red Oak commented as he pulled out his skinning blade and once again looked at the two spears sticking into the chest of the young buffalo.

White Swan thanked Red Oak for mentioning the spring and then signaled to Quite Pheasant to follow her.

"You just asked Grey Fox Running to be your mate, but he did not answer, what now." Quiet Pheasant commented.

"I heard him say yes. He just wants me to smell better than a buffalo," White Swan said as she thought about the position, she had put him in.

You should ask Red Oak, White Swan continued with a chuckle.

White Swan's interpretation was a good one and Quiet Pheasant took her advice and proposed a similar union with Red Oak.

Later they were able to give a positive answer to their father's question.

"Will I be hunting for two mate-less daughters or was the hunt successful," their father asked on their return.

"Look at their faces and you will see your answer," their mother replied as she gave her two daughters a hug.

Quiet Pheasant commented that her shameless sister had extended the proposal to Grey Fox Running and that she had followed her older sister's lead and shamed Red Oak to make a mating proposal as well.

And then we gave the buffalo to the two young men so they could come by and gift our parents with the meat.

White Swan laughed and commented that the rest of the clan meeting would go slowly but she and her sister would be moving into a new clan and have two handsome warriors to hunt with.

THE END

37

Floating Cloud

loating Cloud sat on the lakeside path with her dead daughter on her lap. Silent Pool's last words were "I am with Fast Skimmer. Please take good care of Quiet Rabbit." Then she closed her eyes and with a smile on her lips she let out a long breath and was gone.

Floating Cloud knew that her will to live had left her moons ago when she lost her soul mate.

Floating Cloud looked up into the clear blue sky. Her tears ran freely down her cheeks. She had watched Silent Pool look up and smile, then trip over a limp, fall backward and hit her head on a stone. It was as if she had seen where she was going. Her smile was the first since Fast Skimmer had been killed.

Floating Cloud thought back at her own similar experience. Her parents had not approved of the person she had chosen as her mate. Her mother had sent her on her way declaring that her family name was now Black Storm Cloud.

She and her mate had made their own way for almost twenty moon cycles then they came upon the Elk Hide Clan and had been accepted.

It was an overwhelming shock when, that fall season, she lost her mate during the first hunt. He fell from a cliff as he tried to run down a small boar.

She had been devastated but her love for Silent Pool had sustained her.

Silent Pool was the reason she had recovered. She was born on a spring morning like the one she had now died on. Floating Cloud thought back to all the times her daughter had saved her from the darkness that often threatened to consume her. She knew that she had not been able to give that relief back to Silent Pool.

Now she sat and cried.

She stood and picked up Silent Pool and slowly carried her back to the Elk Campsite. She would take her to the Shaman of the Next Life who would prepare her for the journey to the land of the Ancestors.

White Swan came to her and helped carry Silent Pool. She asked what had happened. She listened as Floating Cloud described what had taken place and her interpretation of it.

White Swan commented on how sad she was. Fast Skimmer had been a good friend and when he and Silent Pool became mates, she too became a good friend.

She shared the fact that it had been clear to everyone how much Silent Pool missed her mate.

White Swan left Floating Cloud with the Shaman but told her to come to her camp site when she was through. She would have Quiet Rabbit there.

Silent Pool had once again given Floating Cloud a reason to stay young. She would need all her strength to care for and raise her grand-daughter Quiet Rabbit. She would need Quiet Rabbit as much as Quiet Rabbit would need her.

When she saw White Swan approaching, Quiet Rabbit knew that something was wrong. When she was invited to have the morning meal at White Swan's campsite, she knew it was bad. She was trembling as she walked with White Swan to her camp.

Taelo was sitting on a log near the fire. He looked at her and pointed to a seat near to him. He pointed to a leather sack hanging near the fire and said that the morning stew would make them all feel better.

Quiet Rabbit looked at Grey Fox Running. He seemed to have the same tears in his eyes that he had on the day he brought her father home.

She immediately had tears in her eyes. She knew instantly that Floating Cloud would come to tell her that her mother was gone.

She began to silently cry.

She felt Taelo's arm go around her shoulder. He gave her a hug and quietly told her his heart hurt too. He told her to look at the clouds in the sky and imaging floating there with her father and mother.

Floating Cloud took in the scene around White Swan's cook fire. She paused for a moment, took a deep breath before going on.

She tried to keep her composure as she approached Quiet Rabbit. She was not sure how she was going to break the news.

Quiet Rabbit looked up at Floating Cloud and saw tears in her eyes. It was clear to her that everyone was crying.

It was also obvious that her mother was not there.

She knew in her heart that her mother was with her father. It was where her mother wished to be.

A shiver ran through her. She closed her eyes and wished her mother happiness.

She looked up at her grandmother and patted the seat next to herself as Taelo had done for her.

She looked around and quietly said what everyone seemed to be avoiding, "My mother is with father. It is as she wished. Later I will want to hear how she made the journey. Now I think it is time we all enjoyed the morning stew."

Floating Cloud was surprised by Quiet Rabbit's immediate understanding and how she handled the situation. She was acting more mature than her twelve seasons' age. She also knew that it would take time for her to really come to terms with the loss of her mother.

She sat down and asked whether the stew was ready. She once again thanked her own mate for having made good friends with Grey Fox Running, White Swan, Quiet Pheasant, White Swan's sister, and Red Oak. She knew they would support her and Quiet Rabbit.

Departing two sun cycles later to go to the clan meeting was a change that both Floating Cloud and Quiet Rabbit needed.

Floating Cloud packed all the things that had been made and prepared for trading. This preparation was more emotional than Floating Clout had anticipated.

Silent Pool had worked hard to prepare for this event. She had many items to trade. She had planned to make this trip and had planned for success.

It was clear to Floating Cloud that her death on the path was an accident. Silent pool had planned to make sure she could raise her daughter just as she had done.

Floating Cloud made a vow to get the best deals possible. It was going to be harder in the future for Quiet Rabbit and her to have this much to trade. They would be on their own and it would be hard for them to accumulate the materials and have the time to make goods to trade.

Little did she know the granddaughter she would raise would be a leader among all the clans.

The journey to the Elk Clan's meeting valley was bordered on each side by mountains and had the effect of allowing the events of the past several moon cycles to dissipate in intensity. The ache would be long. But its leaving would happen, and it would remain at a manageable level.

As they traveled, every morning, Floating Cloud would find a rabbit, ground hog or several squirrels lying outside her enclosure.

She was not sure who the generous person might be, but she had her suspicions. She was pleased that someone was concerned enough to make sure that she and Quiet Rabbit had a good morning meal and that there would be enough for a second meal.

A few sun cycles later she stood with the rest of the clan looking down at the small oblong lake and the valley where all the Elk Clan was gathered for the Elk Clan meeting. The Elk Hide Clan was the last to arrive.

Floating Cloud listened as Taelo suggested that the Elk Hide Clan make their camp on the far side of the lake. Their clan would be the first to camp on the far side. The only thing preventing this had been the need to cross the small river that fed the lake. He proposed putting up a way to walk across.

She was pleased when Wise Owl assigned Taelo the task of leading a team to build a bridge across the stream that fed the lake. He was to signal success to the clan by lighting a fire and sending up white smoke.

When the sun reached the zenith and the white smoke signal rose up into the air, she raised her voice and shouted enthusiastically with the rest of the clan. She knew it would be a good meeting and that she and Quite Rabbit would not be carrying water very far.

She took Quite Rabbit's hand and they marched past all the other sub-clans on their way to a lakeside camp.

She made sure they both were displaying their best trade garments as they walked proudly to their premier campsite.

In the sun cycles that followed, her aggressive trading paid off. She traded for several gorgeous outfits and additional footwear. Each sun cycle she made a visit to the one camp that specialized in snacks and treats. There she would get some small treat for both herself and for Quiet Rabbit.

She was spoiling them both and enjoying it.

The meeting progressed smoothly. Then she learned that Grey Fox Running would be leaving the Elk Hide Clan to become the leader of the original Elk Clan.

Floating Cloud went to White Swan to confirm the rumor she had heard. When White Swan confirmed the change of sub-clan, Floating Cloud immediately asked if she and Quiet Rabbit could join the Elk Clan.

She knew that this change would be good for her as well as for Quiet Rabbit. It would be a fresh start for them both.

She returned to Quiet Rabbit to tell her about the change.

She was again surprised by Quiet Rabbit.

Quiet Rabbit had overheard Taelo and Golden Hawk talking about their move to the Elk Clan.

She immediately wanted to do the same. She did not wish to return to the place where she had lost both her mother and father.

When Floating Cloud approached, the look on her face shouted out that she too wanted to join the Elk Clan.

When Floating Cloud asked whether Quiet Rabbit was interested in joining the Elk Clan, Quiet Rabbit smiled and gave her grandmother a hug and whispered a thank you and a yes.

Once the change of leaders for the Elk Clan was announced, and Grey Fox Running accepted her, Floating Cloud, let Wise Owl know about her desire to change clans.

She felt relieved when Wise Owl agreed with her that it was a good move and would provide a way for both she and Quiet Rabbit to find new happiness.

Her next shock came when all the other clans had left the valley.

Grey Fox Running and Red Oak asked that all the Elk Clan families display their food supply. Except for Grey Fox Running and Red Oak, she had almost as much for her and Quiet Rabbit than all the food the other families possessed.

She realized the Elk Clan was in dire a straight and realized why Silent Hawk, the leader that had brought the Elk Clan to the meeting willingly accepted Grey Fox Running as the immediate leader for the Elk Clan and Red Oak as a lead hunter.

The Elk Clan had lost their lead hunter to a rhino attack. The hunt had gone very badly. The Elk Clan was on the verge of running out of food. They would not last until the winter solstice unless the ancients acted.

She was somewhat alarmed when two-thirds of her food was redistributed to the various clan families. This meant that even by rationing and cutting back she would be out of food by the solstice.

She kept quiet because she trusted that Grey Fox Running and Red Oak would successfully guide the Elk Clan, but she worried. She did not have a hunter to resupply her.

Floating Cloud was surprised that the rabbits and other small game kept appearing at her cook fire. This was a great comfort to her.

When each morning the food for the day was at her cooking ring, it was clear that the person she suspected was now with her in the Elk Clan. This gave her new hope.

When Taelo came in with the news that he and Golden Hawk had found a large hive of honeybees, Floating Cloud gave a sigh of relief.

Taelo and Golden Hawk seemed to be single handedly giving the Elk Clan reason to believe that they would survive the cold weather that had engulfed them. The honey was abundant, and all the families received a share.

The elk and deer left on the trail by Brave Deer's hunting party was the next event that signaled to the clan that they would most likely survive the winter.

Floating Cloud tried to catch her benefactor in the act of leaving the rabbits and other small game at her campfire, but it was clear that she was not going to catch that person in the act.

Not many sun cycles later, as they passed a valley branching off to the side of the direction of the clan's travel, an eagle's cry came from the air.

White Swan insisted that the Elk Clan stop and make camp early. She insisted Taelo and Golden Hawk, who had left the clan to scout the surrounding area, were facing some trial and they might need help.

Floating Cloud vocally supported White Swan. Quiet Pheasant was also insistent. It was clear to Silent Hawk, who, in Grey Fox Running's absence, was temporarily leading the clan, that he would have little choice. He did the wise thing and called for an early halt.

When late in the night, Taelo and Golden Hawk returned, Floating Cloud and Quiet Rabbit were among the first to help them pull the travois carrying a large elk and two enormous dire wolf skins.

The wolf skins were so large that at first the old hunters thought the hides might be bear hides. Two wolves of the size of the hides would have easily defeated two skilled hunters. They wondered how two hunters as young and inexperienced as Taelo and Golden Hawk could possibly have killed them.

Floating Cloud offered to treat the hides and make a coat and vest for Taelo and Golden Hawk.

White Swan thanked her and accepted the offer. She jokingly asked what Floating Cloud would do with the second hide.

The next morning instead of rabbit or some other small game, her suspicion was confirmed when she instead found a large block of elk meat by her cook fire.

She never had any doubt about who had been leaving her the food but now she wondered how he was able to do so and never be seen.

A few sun cycles later the clan arrived at the seaside.

It was clear to her by Taelo and Golden Hawk's frozen leggings that they had been to the sea ahead of the clan.

She offered both of them a dry set of newly made dire wolf skin clothing. Taelo smiled and thanked her for being so kind and took her up on the offer.

White Swan watched as Taelo accepted the dire wolf long pants. She too had noticed the frozen pants both he and Golden Hawk were in.

She walked over to Taelo and complimented him on the dire wolf outfit just as he was putting on the matching jacket. She felt the soft inner lining of the jacket and looked over at Floating Cloud with her eyebrows raised. She whispered what a jacket and thanked her for doing such excellent work and doing it so quickly.

Silent Hawk surprised the Elk Clan members by asking White Swan to scout down the coast for a suitable winter camp for the clan. He would go up the coast and do the same.

If a suitable location was found the clan was to follow the first team that returned and begin to immediately set up the camp.

Floating Cloud was not surprised when White Swan quickly accepted and asked Quiet Pheasant to be her partner. Nor was she surprised when Taelo and Golden Hawk both said they were also going.

She took note that the two had not asked but declared their participation. The two were already demonstrating the leadership that she had recognized in them.

She was surprised when she volunteered but was rejected. White Swan thanked her but told her to get everyone ready to follow her when she returned.

Two sun cycles later Floating Cloud watched as the four returned. White Swan and Quiet Pheasant were moving at a good jogging pace, but it was clear that Taelo and Golden Hawk were having no problem keeping that pace.

She was sure the two younger members could easily out pace their mothers.

Floating Cloud listened as various Elk Clan members resisted following White Swan to the location she had found.

She picked up her belongings and loudly declared she was ready to follow White Swan. She watched as one of the shy young Elk Clan young women followed her lead.

White Swan turned, ordered the Clan to follow and went down the beach. She never looked back.

Floating Cloud and Quiet Rabbit kept up a tally of the number that were following. Finally, they announced that every person on the beach was following.

White Swan and Quiet Pheasant fell back and thanked each person for following them. Floating Cloud listened as they gave a work assignment to each person. The two had already picked the location for the large clan lodge and had determined that the digging and material collection would begin when they arrived at the site.

When they arrived at the location, Floating Cloud immediately fell in love with it.

There was a spit, made up of a tall craggily cliff curving out to sea. It had a monstrous round boulder opposite the cliff that created a quiet inner cove. There was a flat beach area that ran back to a cliff where the entire clan could set up their camp.

She immediately staked out her choice for her campsite near a small, sweet water stream that made its way across the beach to the foot of spit cliffs.

She concluded that it would be the best camp that she had experienced in her lifetime.

White Swan's immediate push to erect a central clan lodge enrolled every able-bodied person.

Quiet Rabbit commented that she had never worked so hard. Floating Cloud gave her a hug and asked if they had made the right choice?

Quiet Rabbit replied that she would not want it any other way.

Silver Hawk returned as the main lodge took its final shape. Every hide had been used to create a warm enclosure but the homes for individual families would have to wait until the three long hunt teams returned.

Floating Cloud listened as Silver Hawk praised White Swan's leadership and the clan members for the hard work. It was clear to her that White Swan had been raised to a new level of respect.

Floating Cloud had copied the in-ground design used for the lodge to build her hutch. She and Quiet Rabbit had dug out and built a snug hutch that provided them enough room for each to have their sleeping area on opposite sides and a back area to store their personal goods. They had made the walls of stone and had put the main cross member poles across the tops of the stone wall that was about half their height above the ground. Since they had no large animal hides, they had woven small willow branches into a mat and had covered the mat with grass.

The two had given each other a hug when they put the last bundle of grass into place. They both commented that it would keep out the snow and the cold but wondered if in the spring it would keep out the rain.

A small fire at the entrance kept the interior warm.

They shared their design with the rest of the clan, but a hard snow presented a barrier for the other families to dig and build something similar. Floating Cloud knew that they had been lucky to get their hutch done.

She was relieved when Brave Deer and his hunting group returned. But the physical condition of the hunters was a shock. Their tale of being attacked by a pack of dire wolves put new fear in her heart about the forest and animals around them. She was reminded of Taelo's and Golden Hawk's encounter with dire wolves that she now figured had attacked Brave Deer and his hunters.

She again thought about the two and realized that they had on their own passed the test of being hunters and warriors.

She was glad to be on the isolated beach front that was protected on three sides. Her enthusiasm for building a wall from the beach back to the cliff, as suggested by White Swan, went up dramatically. It seemed to her that everyone else had the same reaction.

A moon cycle later Red Oak and his hunters returned with four heavily load travois of meat. Floating Cloud and Quiet Rabbit listened as he told of the attack of a band of Others.

Floating Cloud was disturbed by this tale.

She listened as White Swan and Quiet Pheasant discussed their plan to address the presence of a Clan of Others up the coast. She agreed with them that an approach showing concern and kindness would work better than a show of force. She had heard that the Others were very ferocious fighters.

Once again, she was turned down when she volunteered to go along with White Swan. She understood the rejection but she none the less wanted to show her support in a direct way.

When resistance was voiced by some clan members, she openly and publicly praised White Swan for such a level-headed approach.

She and Quiet Rabbit were on the beach and watched as White Swan, Quiet Pheasant, Golden Hawk and Taelo left with their food and gift loaded travois.

Silver Hawk had yielded to White Swan. He stood next to Floating Cloud and commented that the women of the clan were clearly as brave as any of the hunters and warriors.

It was only three sun cycles later as she and Quiet Rabbit sat on their favorite beach side boulder that they saw White Swan and Quiet Pheasant jogging toward them. They were by themselves.

Floating Cloud's initial concern about the absence of Taelo and Golden Hawk dissipated when she watched the relaxed way White Swan and Quiet Pheasant were moving and conversing.

She turned to Quiet Rabbit and commented that they would ask about Taelo and Golden Hawk but that it was clear there was no trouble.

White Swan's tale of her meeting with the Clan of Others and Taelo knocking out a huge young man had the Elk Clan members spell bound. The fact that the Others had been waiting for Taelo was a surprise.

Floating Cloud remembered the Naming Day when Taelo had selected the claw of an eagle and the eagle that had been circling for the entire time made a steep dive and plucked the claw from his up stretched hand.

It turned out that event had somehow become part of the Clan of Others heritage.   He had been expected but the fact that he was a members of the New Ones had surprised the Others.

She and Quiet Rabbit made good use of the large elk hide given them by Red Oak before his departure to get Grey Fox Running. They oiled it and stretched it over their woven mat of branches that made up the roof of their hutch.

They immediately experienced a new warm interior.   They were now certain that the spring rains would be kept out.

It was only a few sun cycles later when after the sun had dipped below the far horizon.   She and Quiet Rabbit were still sitting on their favorite shore side boulder when White Swan let out the eagle cry that she used to identify herself to her family.

Two replies came back.

Grey Fox Running and his hunters were approaching with several travois of meat.   The surprise was that Taelo, and Golden Hawk had returned at the same time.

The bigger surprise was that they were escorted by four warriors of the Others.

Floating Cloud hugged Quiet Rabbit as they watched Grey Fox Running greet the Others and invite them into the Elk Clans Home.

She learned that the huge Other warrior, whose name was Burley Bear, was the person Taelo had knocked out.   That event had bonded Burley Bear to Taelo.

Winter hit hard.

The weather became a challenge and the cold crept in along the floor and chilled one's feet. She and Quiet Rabbit huddled by their warming fire.

They had moved it to the center of their hutch and made an opening in the roof above it. Even so they each wore a rabbit skin vest and had on rabbit skin lined knee-high boots.

They learned of Taelo's and Golden Hawk's departure on the morning that they watched Burley Bear climb the cliff as he went out to find them.

Floating Cloud wondered out loud why the two would pick the heart of a cold winter to do such a thing.

Quiet Rabbit replied that they were probably responding to a call from the Ancients.

Floating Cloud worried as the weather became worse and the cold became threatening. She worried about where Taelo and Golden Hawk might find shelter.

Her other concern was about the clan's food supply. She had listened to Grey Fox Running comment on the potential need to send out a group of hunters when the weather improved.

She made sure the two of them had one good meal every morning. She kept a hot stew by the fire for the afternoon meal. They were both losing weight. Everyone in camp was having the same problem.

Several moon cycles later, when she and Quiet rabbit could count the few number of sun cycles of food they had left, a scout came and let Grey Fox Running know that strangers were coming toward them along the beach from the south.

Quiet Rabbit grabbed her hand and together they followed Grey Fox Running to the top of the spit cliffs.

On the way to the top of the cliff she heard Quiet Rabbit comment that she was sure it was Taelo returning.

Floating Cloud had no idea how Quiet Rabbit would have known that it was Taelo, but she was right.

The entire Elk Clan celebrated the return of all three young hunters who had pulled back a sled loaded with three young buffalo. Even better they had brought the news that the buffalo herd spent their winter in what the three had named the Valley of Plenty.

The Elk Clan now had ample food and therefore of hides.

Spring brought out the small blue and yellow flowers on the side of the spit's cliffs. Their campsite was warmed by the sun and Floating Cloud experienced new energy. The sea, the cliffs and the warm sun gave the entire clan a feeling of well-being.

When Taelo and Golden Hawk began building their fish trap she enthusiastically supported Quiet Rabbit and her two new friends Busy Bee and Talking Wren as they organized the younger clan members to help build the trap.

She was not surprised at the success of the fish trap and the fact that it engaged the entire Elk Clan as the fish were caught, processed, and dried. She had been present when a much younger Taelo had changed how the Elk Hide Clan had captured their spring salmon with a much smaller version of the trap that was now in the bay.

She was astounded when Taelo, Golden Hawk and Burley Bear killed a giant shark that had entered the fish trap. It was so large that the shark was processed like it was a buffalo.

She and a group of volunteers stretched the shark skin for processing. She let White Swan know that she would use the shark skin as White Swan desired.

She reinforced Taelo's public recognition of Quiet Rabbit, Busy Bee, and Talking Wren for their contribution in building the fish trap. He gave them the best and most teeth, but he had shared the teeth with all the clan members.

Floating Cloud commented to Quiet Rabbit that the generosity shown by the Taelo, Golden Hawk and Burley Bear spoke of their high character.

Quiet Rabbit smiled and put her hand to her heart but said nothing.

The fishing was so successful that it was reduced to only a few hours a day.

A flat stone area along the spit was turned into a salt making area. She and Quiet Rabbit claimed a square that was two spear lengths long. Each day they would carefully scrape off the dried white sea salt and then put more salt water on their square. The sun then did the job of evaporating the water and making a new layer of salt.

Floating Cloud was relieved by the fact that she and Quiet Rabbit were not going to be destitute.

They would have a very large supply of salt. They had a very large supply of dried fish. They ate fresh fish or meat each day.

And Quiet Rabbit and her two friends had become the supplier of small game and a variety of roots and berries.

Floating Cloud commented on their success and complemented Quiet Rabbit for her ability to supply so much food.

The spit was the home of thousands of seagulls and other birds. She and Quiet Rabbit gathered many eggs for their meals.

The spit was also covered in blueberries. The two of them gathered berries to eat fresh but they also cooked them and made a jam that could be kept for future use and to trade.

Floating Cloud felt a warmth flow through her when White Swan suggested that Quiet Rabbit should volunteer to go on a long hunt with Taelo and Golden Hawk.

She asked if any other young women would go as well.

White Swan let her know that she was making the same suggestion to Busy Bee and Talking Wren. These were Quiet Rabbits best friends.

Floating Cloud knew the answer to her question to Quiet Rabbit by the look of pleasure she saw.

She gave Quiet Rabbit a hug and told her that it would be an adventure of a lifetime.

Not long after the hunt began, she watched as Little Beaver and Talking Wren returned with a young bull pulling a travois loaded with a huge supply of meat.

The novelty of an animal pulling a travois and the amount of meat that the team had sent back impressed the entire Clan.

The story of the first hunt and how both Taelo, hunting with Quiet Rabbit, Golden Hawk, hunting with Busy Bee had each killed four buffalo in one hunt, had Floating Cloud feeling like her name.   She knew that Quiet Rabbit had wanted to hunt with Taelo. She knew Quiet Rabbit's intent and approved.

She noticed that both White Swan and Quiet Pheasant had smiles as they looked at each other.

Floating Cloud complemented Little Otter and Talking Wren and sent a sack full of honey for the team to enjoy.

Floating Cloud publicly made the point that the team, the leaders had predicted would do poorly, had outperformed the other hunt teams many times over.

She was not going to let the leaders forget their negative view of the women of the clan being hunting partners.

The return of the hunters led by Little Otter and the four meat loaded travois that by themselves was more than the other three long hunt teams had brought in sealed Floating Cloud's assessment of Taelo's and Golden Hawk's hunting skill.

Floating Cloud also took in who was walking with whom. Quiet Rabbit was at Taelo's side, Busy Bee was at Golden Hawk's side and Talking Wren was talking to Little Otter.

She knew that Quite Pool, looking down from the land of the Ancients would be pleased.

A few sun cycles later she was sitting with White Swan and Quiet Pheasant. The sun was on its way to kiss the sea at its horizon.

Taelo, Quiet Rabbit, Golden Hawk and Busy Bee were walking along the beach and talking to each other.

Both White Swan and Quiet Pheasant wistfully commented on the scene and the fact that their sons seemed have decided on their mates.

Floating Cloud smiled and commented that it was reassuring when soulmate met soulmate and wasn't this what the two of them had wanted.

The End

63

Quiet Rabbit

Quiet Rabbit walked slowly behind and took in the orange, yellow and red of the leaves. The bright red leaves on one bush caught her eye and she wondered what name it had. She ran her hand through the tan waving grasses. She looked into a cloudless sky at a lone eagle gliding in a graceful seemingly effortless dance with the wind.

She pulled her favorite jacket snuggly around her as the gust reminded her that the season was chilling, and the cold season was ahead.

She had fallen behind as she absorbed what to her were the wonders of her world. She hurried forward to catch up with her parents.

They were holding hands and talking quietly to each other. Quiet Rabbit could not hear what they were saying but it did not matter. The way they were walking, the way they were talking, and the way they looked at each other was what Quiet Rabbit absorbed.

She knew that the bond, the force, the way they were one, was what she wanted for herself.   To her it seemed that the two reinforced each other and together they were powerful, they were whole.   She felt the warmth as if the two harbored the flames of a fire.

Quiet Rabbit ran ahead past them, until she reached a rocky open area along the lake bank.   She looked around for some flat rocks that she could skip across the water.   She giggled as her skipping stone was passed by one that went much farther than hers.

Her father had been given the name Flat Stone at his naming ceremony after he selected a flat stone from the edge of the naming blanket, but he was now known as Fast Skimmer for the speed of his running and his ability to skip his stones farther than anyone in the Elk Clan.   He was also one of the best hunters in the Clan.

He was friends with Red Oak and Grey Fox Running.   The three were the lead hunters for the clan.

He had told her mother and her that this was his departure walk with the two most beautiful women in his life.

He, Red Oak and Gray Fox Running were taking the hunters out on a long hunt.   The Clan needed a fresh supply of meat to make it through the coming cycle.   The hunters would be gone for at least one moon.

She felt the exhilaration flow through her as he picked her up and spun around with her in the air.   They laughed together for the whole time.

The evening ended with them sitting together around White Swan's fire and sharing stories of long hunts in the past and of past exploits that they had shared.

The next day her father, Grey Fox Running and Red Oak led the hunting parties out for their annual long hunt.   They would bring back enough meat to feed the Elk Horn Clan until the warm season.

She and her mother both wished all the hunters good hunting. The better the hunt went, the sooner the hunters came home.

Their return would be the trigger to prepare to travel to the seasonal gathering of all the Elk sub-clans.

The sun cycles seemed long and the moon cycles even longer. Finally, a runner came in with the news that the long hunters were returning.

She and her mother had marked a stick each evening as the sun left for the night and yielded to the sky lit by the twinkling of the many ancestors and the huge white lady of the night.   They laughed together about the fact that they were Fast Skimmer's beautiful women, but he was their strong handsome man.

She and her mother spent many hours preparing goods that could be traded at the fall clan gathering.

A scout had returned and let the Clan know that the long hunters were returning. She and her mother and the rest of the Clan stood at the edge of the village waiting for their arrival.

A cheer went up when everyone saw at least six heavily loaded travois being pulled toward them.

Quiet Rabbit scanned the entire convoy but did not see the figure she was searching for. She looked up at her mother when the hand on her shoulder began to squeeze her to the point it hurt.

She had never seen her mother's face look so colorless. She took in the tears running down her face mother's face. Then her mother pushed her away and began to run toward the returning hunters.

Quiet Rabbit did not know what was wrong, but she ran after her mother. She had her father's running skill and easily caught up. She did not understand but a deep fear rose up and almost choked her.

Her mother ran toward Grey Fox Running.

Quiet Rabbit saw him turn and say something to Red Oak and then stepped aside to let the returning hunters proceed toward the camp.

She watched as her mother briefly looked at Red Oak and then continued to run towards Grey Fox Running.

There was one lone travois being pulled in the last position. The person pulling the travois stopped and put it down as her mother approached.

Grey Fox Running signaled for the hunter to go on.

Her mother knelt and slowly untied the elk skin wrapped around the figure. She reached out and touched the elk skin. She noted that the elk skin had been processed and felt soft and smooth.

The fur had been turned inward as was the custom. She knew that the spirit within was to be treated gently.

Her mother looked up at Grey Fox Running and thanked him for the respect that had been shown to Fast Skimmer.

Quiet Rabbit watched as her mother, true to her name cried silently as she leaned forward to put her hand on her father's face.

Tears were running down her own cheek as she stood frozen in her tracks. She welcomed the strong hands that lifted her.

She looked directly into Grey Fox Running's eyes and was surprised to see tears. He was a warrior, a hunter but he had lost one of his lifelong friends and he had to be the one to share this with his friend's mate and daughter.

She felt a surge of emptiness. A void filled her mind. She was glad that Grey Fox Running kept holding her.

Quiet Rabbit watched as White Swan and Floating Cloud arrived and comforted her mother. White Swan urged her mother to walk with her back to camp. Floating Cloud closed the elk skin cover and Grey Fox Running pulled the travois and followed the women.

******

The next moon cycle was one of the hardest Quiet Rabbit could remember. Her mother would not talk. She would walk most of the day and cry.

Quiet Rabbit went to her grandmother, Floating Cloud, seeking understanding and company.

Floating Cloud told her the story of how she too had lost her mate. At that time, she was pregnant with Silent Pool. Her husband, Proud Cougar, had gone fishing and had accidently been in the territory of a brown bear. He had only his fishing knife to defend himself, but he had killed the bear. In the ferocious fight he was mortally wounded.

He had staggered back to their camp carrying the fish he had gone to catch for dinner. He died in her arms, shortly after making it back.

****

Floating Cloud assured Quiet Rabbit that her mother would recover.

Immediately after the story, Quiet Rabbit went back to her mother and gave her a hug. She knew how hard it must be for her mother to have lost her soul mate.

Silent Pool was determined to overcome her grief. She had a daughter to care for but the grief, like the black of night, would come to the surface to pull her into the dark.

She would lose track of time. She would lose herself as she went about her daily chores. She worked exceptionally hard to prepare for the Elk clan gathering. She knew that she had to have enough goods so that she could take care of her daughter.

She knew she had to recover.   The clan would soon leave for the seasonal clan meeting.   For the sake of Quiet Rabbit, she had to make sure the family remained in good standing.

One morning, Silent Pool decided to get fresh water to make a rabbit stew for the morning meal.   Stew always helped her to face the day.   She asked her mother to go to the lake with her.

The sun was rising behind her and up ahead the clear pool of water awaited her.   She looked up at the clear blue sky.   It reminded her of her last walk with Fast Skimmer.   A smile came to her lips, she turned to let her mother know about her memory, but she tripped on a windblown limb and staggered and fell backwards.   She still had as smile on her lips as her head hit a fist sized stone.

Floating Cloud had been several paces behind Silent Pool and watched her trip and hit her head.   She rushed forward and cradled her in her arms.

Silent Pool briefly opened her eyes, quietly muttered the words, "I am with him.   Take good care of her."   She then closed her eyes and let out a long breath.   In a rapid instance, she was gone!

****

Floating Cloud sat with Silent Pool's head on her lap and quietly cried.   She knew that Silent Pool had gone to where she wanted to be.

She would need to gently let Quiet Rabbit know.   She promised herself that she would take care of Quiet Rabbit like she was her own daughter.

Quiet Rabbit woke as the sun touched her cheek and warmed it.   She shielded her eyes to see if her mother was out by the cooking fire.

She got up and walked out hoping to get something to eat. No one was about.

She went to her grandmother's shelter, but it was empty.

White Swan walked up and told her to come to her camp breakfast.

Quiet Rabbit knew immediately that something bad had happened.

Taelo was sitting by the fire ring and patted the seat next to him.

A few moments later her grandmother, appeared as she came back from having left Silent Pool with the clan's seer.   He would prepare her for her trip to the ancients.

Quiet Rabbit took one look and knew that her grandmother had news she did not want to hear.

The loss of her father had saddened Quiet Rabbit.   He had been her play partner.   The loss of her mother broke her heart. Her mother had been her comforter and confident.

Quiet Rabbit felt so alone.

Floating Cloud shared Silent Pool's last words and hugged Quiet Rabbit.

****

Two sun cycles later the clan left for the annual Elk Clan gathering.

Quiet Rabbit knew that the Elk clan now boasted seven prospering sub-clans.

Her father had told her that the success of the Clan was due in large part to solid leaders, to their hunters and to a group of elders, who brought balance to the hotter heads. It was also due to their willingness to share their resources to balance out the vital food stores prior to each winter. Ensuring each clan had enough food for the winter was one of the most critical tasks during the meeting.

She knew that for the last several seasons the Elk Horn Clan had out produced all the other clans by a significant amount. They had generously shared food supplies with the other sub-clans.

This year the Elk Horn clan was loaded with an over-abundance of dried fish, elk, rabbit, moose, and other food stuffs. Their supply of leather goods, baskets, general utensils, woven cloth, various tools, fishhooks, stone ax heads and clothing made them the most prosperous members of the clan. This abundance had so loaded them down that they were the last to arrive at the meeting valley.

Her mother had prepared well. She had told Quiet Rabbit that the two of them would need to be hard traders. They now had to make their own way.

****

Quiet Rabbit took in the scene below them.

The early morning was still. All was quiet. The light wispy campfire smoke from each family camp rose straight into the still morning air like white worms dancing slowly in the wind. The undulation of the parallel plumes of smoke seemed to be orchestrated as they danced in unison. The sun, rising over the far horizon caused them to change colors of pinks and yellows and it seemed as if the plumes were alive.

The Wise Owl their leader stopped at the top of the hill to look out across the valley.

It was a scene that caused everyone in the Elk Horn Clan to stop and take in the beauty.

Quiet Rabbit immediately took in the grouping of campfires. It indicated all the other sub clans, but theirs, had already arrived and set up camp. The Elk Horn Clan would have to take the place farthest away from the river and up along the hillside.

Wise Owl stood overlooking the valley below. She heard him comment that he really disliked having arrived so late.

Because of their abundant wealth, it had taken them longer to pack up and they had traveled slower than anticipated because of their load. Now he stood contemplating what he should have his sub clan do.

Quiet Rabbit stood with her grandmother taking in the sight of the Elk Clan gathering.

She listened as Taelo suggested they camp on the other side of the lake.   None of the Elk sub clans had ever camped there because of the small stream feeding the lake.

He pointed out the advantages and was given the task of build a bridge across the stream and then signaling success.

Wise Owl decided to give it a try.   He liked the idea of walking by all the camp sites showing off his Clan's richness and then proceeding to an excellent campsite on the edge of the lake.

He gave Taelo the task to build a bridge across the stream and then signal success via a fire with green leaves thrown in to send up a white plume.

Later she watched as the signal, set by Taelo and his team of bridge builders, rose into the air and signaled that the other side was ready for the Elk Horn Clan.

She along with the rest of the Elk Hide Clan let out a loud hurrah.   It made her feel so good.   She would long remember having her spirit uplifted.

She and her Grandmother walked proudly through the Elk camp and across to the other side of the lake.

Both had a great supply of goods to trade and looked forward to the gathering and the bartering that would take place.

A few sun cycles later, Floating Cloud asked her if she were willing to leave the Elk Horn Clan and move into the Elk clan. She went on to explain that Grey Fox Running was to be the new leader of the Elk Clan and that she thought it would be good for the two of them to change clans and join the Elk Clan.

Though very surprised, Quiet Rabbit immediately agreed. One of her best friends was Grey Fox Running's son. She wanted to be where he was, and she did not want to go back to the place that would constantly remind her of her father's and mother's death.

The change of clan to the original parent Elk Clan was a welcome one for her. It took her away from the sorrow she associated with the Elk Hide Clan.

The fact that she and all Elk Clan members were immediately on food rations was a surprise that alarmed her.

Most of the food that she and her grandmother had accumulated through hard trading was distributed to each of the Elk Clan families by Grey Fox Running and Red Oak.

Every person in the Clan had about the same amount of food. Quiet Rabbit knew that the amount would not be enough to take them through the coming cold cycle.

The journey to their new home was to be long and challenging.

She watched as Taelo and Golden Hawk became the inspiration for the young members of the Elk Clan.

She did not go out to hunt and scout as they did, but she organized those who stayed with the moving caravan, to gather berries and to fish the streams and small lakes they were passing.

She in her own right gained the respect of the Elk Clan members. White Swan was like an aunt to her and encouraged her efforts.

She found the journey to the coast long and tedious.

Taelo and Golden Hawk broke the tediousness when they found the honey tree. The entire Elk Clan gathered around the very large twisted and exceptionally knurled oak tree. The amount of honey exceeded anything that had been experienced before.

High overhead an eagle let out a loud cry.

Quite Rabbit soon came to know each time a special event was happening to Taelo. An eagle would fly overhead and let out a long cry.

She was there listening when White Swan, Taelo's mother insisted the clan stop and wait for Taelo to return from an excursion he and Golden Hawk had taken. White Swan explained that the cry of the eagle meant that Taelo was experiencing a special event.

Late that night, as the Elk Clan waited, Taelo and Golden Hawk entered camp pulling a travois loaded with a large elk and the hides of two exceptionally large dire wolves.

The elk provided the margin of food that relieved the leaders concern about feeding the clan for the near term.

She helped White Swan and her grandmother as they fed Taelo and Golden Hawk.

She was amazed as she listened to their account of fighting three very large dire wolves. She heard some of the old-seasoned hunters of the clan say that what the two had done was almost impossible.

****

Two sun cycles later, four hunters from Red Oak's hunting group brought the meat from a buffalo, two boar, four elk and the meat of numerous small game. She and the entire Elk Clan greeted them. It was now clear they would have enough food to continue their journey.

She hid with Taelo and Golden Hawk under a hide so they could stay up and listen to the stories about hunting with Red Oak. She had tears in her eyes because her father had hunted with Red Oak and had told many similar tales, as the one she now listened to.

****

The journey to the coast took longer than Quiet Rabbit had expected. When they finally arrived, Silent Hawk the acting clan leader, while Grey Fox Running was out on the long hunt asked White Swan to go down the coast to look for a good winter camp. Everyone else would stay camped in their current location.

He would go up the coast and do the same.

Whoever found a good location would come back and lead the Elk Clan to their winter home.

Quiet Rabbit watched as White Swan, her sister Quiet Pheasant, Taelo and Golden Hawk jogged away down the beach.

She knew that it was a special situation for a woman to be given such respect and authority.

White Swan returned a few sun cycles later and let the clan know that she had found an excellent home location.

There was confusion when a group said they should wait for Silent Hawk to return before deciding what to do.

White Swan told them to follow her, turned and walked back down the beach.

Quiet Rabbit grabbed her grandmother. They were among the first to follow White Swan to Elk Clan's new home location.

White Swan guided the planning, locating, and building of the main lodge and arranging the layout of the camp.

This was a period that Quiet Rabbit worked harder than she had ever done before. It was a period where everyone was needed to contribute to getting ready to survive the winter.

****

The main lodge was just completed when Red Oak returned with his long hunt team. He told of his encounter with a group of raiding hunters from the people called the Others.

This alarmed the Elk Clan Members.

Quite Rabbit observed that White Swan did not seem to have the same reaction.

A short time later a very battered group of long hunters led by Brave Dear returned. They had no additional food. Instead, they told the story of being hunted by a large pack of dire wolves.

Quiet Rabbit looked over at Taelo and Golden Hawk and again wondered how the two had bested the dire wolves. The two had gone up the very valley that Brave Dear and his group had traveled and had probably met part of the same pack of dire wolves.

****

Though opposed by many of the Elk clan elders, White Swan convinced them that she should go and meet with the clan of Others.

White Swan, Quiet Pheasant, Taelo and Golden Hawk took a travois loaded with food and gifts and went north along the coast.

Quiet Rabbit shouted encouragement as the four left the camp.   She held a deep belief that Taelo's and Golden Hawk's presence would be the deciding factor.

Quiet Rabbit and her grandmother kept a daily watch out to the north along the beach. She was at first alarmed as she watched White Swan and Quiet Pheasant returning alone along the beach.

She rushed out to greet them and was greatly relieved when she was told that Taelo and Golden Hawk had been received like heroes.   Later she laughed heartedly when White Swan shared the story of Taelo defending her against a rude and rough bear of a man.

****

The approaching winter solstice brought so many memories of long ago.   Quiet Rabbit had kept herself busy and engaged in preparing the winter camp.   Now she found herself at an emotional low point.   She talked quietly to Floating Cloud about her grief.

Then, she heard the scream of the eagle, not from the sky but out along the beach.

She dropped everything and ran out to the edge of the camp.

The scene was confusing.

Red Oak and Grey Fox Running and the long hunters were gathered in one group.

The Elk Clan members were standing behind White Swan.

And out by a large log were two smaller figures in front of four very powerful looking men of the Others.

Quiet Rabbit watched as the groups converged and greeted each other.   She knew that something very unusual was occurring.

The winter solstice went from a low feeling to a high one.

Her best friend was back.

Her mood changed and she enjoyed the winter solstice much more than she had thought possible.

A moon cycle after the Solstice she learned that Taelo and Golden Hawk had secretly left the camp.   Their new friend and protector, Burly Bear of the Others had followed them in hopes of helping them.

Quiet Rabbit listened to Floating Cloud, White Swan and Quiet Pheasant talking around the cooking fire as they discussed the actions of Taelo and Golden Hawk.

She agreed with them when they highlighted that Burly Bear going out to find his two friends made all of them feel better.

It was hard for her not to worry about the two.   The moon cycles passed slowly.   More than two moon cycles had passed since Taelo left the camp.   The members of the Elk Clan were once again facing a food shortage.

Quiet Rabbit discussed the situation with Floating Cloud. She wondered what she could do to help. She started going out with her sling and she would periodically bring back a rabbit or squirrel.

It was not much but it provided the occasional good meal. She gained confidence in her ability to provide food for herself and her grandmother as her skill with the sling slowly improved.

She was near to Grey Fox Running's camp when a scout came in and said there were people coming in along the coast from the south.

She and her grandmother were standing next to Grey Fox Running at the top of the spit cliffs, when he laughed and said that it could only be Burly Bear, Golden Hawk and Taelo.

She was among the group that went out to greet the returning three. She realized that the meat that was on their sled would tide the whole clan through the coming spring.

Spring was a welcome relief from one of the coldest winters the clan had experienced. Spring was always a frustrating season in that food remained scarce. But Taelo let everyone know that a herd of buffalo spent the cold season in the valley on the other side of the mountains.

****

Quiet Rabbit was among the first supporters when Taelo and Golden Hawk began building a seaside version of their famous fish trap. She organized all the younger members of the camp.

She, her new friends Busy Bee and Talking Wren, became the task masters of getting the necessary long poles and weaving the wooden barrier walls ready to be installed.

The success of the fish trap was an unexpected reward for the Elk Clan. Food became abundant.

The capture of a very large shark in the fish trap made Taelo, Golden Hawk and Burley Bear very affluent young men. The hide was very valuable and each of the very large shark teeth were more valuable than a person's weight in salt.

She, Busy Bee, and Talking Wren were each given three shark teeth. Each got a large one, a medium size and a smaller one. They all knew that they had been singled out and recognized for having given the effort their support.

Quiet Rabbit looked at the three shark teeth given to her by Taelo. She took them and showed them proudly to Floating Cloud who agreed with Taelo that Quiet Rabbit had earned them.

****

The summer season proved to be as generous as Taelo.

The cliff that projected out into the ocean and was the home to thousands of birds yielded not only an abundance of eggs but blueberries as well.

The flat stone area along the cliff base became a place to evaporate the salt water and make salt.

The Elk Clan produced more sea salt than she had ever seen in one place. She, Busy Bee, and Talking Wren had their own salt making area that they managed. They became wealthy salt owners.

Quiet Rabbit led both the egg hunting and blueberry picking. She helped Floating Cloud make a jam of the blue berries by slowly cooking out most of the water and adding a small amount of honey.

****

She was surprised when she, Busy Bee and Talking Wren were approached by White Swan and Quiet Pheasant and told that they should consider going on the long hunt with Taelo and Golden Hawk.

The thought of going on a long hunt thrilled her and her friends.

To go on a long hunt with Taelo was beyond what she could have dreamt of.

A few sun cycles later the long hunt teams were organized. The elders had agreed to one additional long hunt team.   It would have three women on that team.

They named Little Otter as the leader of that team.

Quite Rabbit was surprised at the choice of leader.   Taelo and Golden Hawk both were better leaders than Little Otter.   She looked at both and knew that though the team was being discounted the two were quiet but looking confident.

The long hunt teams left camp.

Taelo commented that their team had been given the worst location.

Burley Bear spoke up and said that he would need to go by the camp of the Others to pick up some of his hunting gear.

Though nothing was said, Quiet Rabbit immediately knew that Burley Bear, Taelo and Golden Hawk were guiding the team in a new direction. She was not sure what they were doing but she knew Burley Bear already had all the hunting gear he needed.

Quiet Rabbit was surprised to have the entire clan of Others out waiting for their hunt team. She watched as Taelo walked up to a badly damaged old man and gave him hug.

Taelo introduced the long hunt team to Broken Spear, the seer of the Others. He also introduced Silver Arrow as the leader of the Others.

Quiet Rabbit walked up and gave Broken Spear a hug just like Taelo had given. She put her hand on the shoulder of Silver Arrow and added her name. She was surprised that he smelled faintly of pine and lavender.

Busy Bee and Talking Wren followed her lead.

She was amazed by the large cave found by Taelo for the Clan of Others. It was more of an open area that looked out at an expansive valley from under the mountain, than a cave.

A waterfall poured cold water into a hot spring basin. The result was a warm water pool. This was a luxury she wished was available to the Elk clan.

Taelo led the team out to it and proceeded to get in and enjoy the hot water.

Quiet Rabbit was the first to join in.

The team was not only welcomed but enjoyed a celebration evening dinner and a long story-telling session.   Taelo and Golden Hawk told stories about each other and about Burley Bear.

It was clear by the hooting and stomping that the Clan enjoyed the stories that made fun of Burley Bear.

The tight bond that existed among her and the rest of the Elk hunters grew to a new depth for Quiet Rabbit.

She was where she wanted to be.

Broken Spear and Silver Arrow, the leader of the others informed the team that Meadow Flower, the future mate of Burley Bear was joining the team.

This, they added, assured that each person and their mate would be on the same long hunt team.

Quiet Rabbit was surprised by the statement but took this as a sign that she would need to act to assure she got the right mate.

She knew she was on the right team, now she was going to make sure she ended up with the right mate.

The team left the cave of the others to hunt in part of the clan's hunting ground.

Broken Spear had warned Taelo that the team faced an unknown challenge and that they would help one of the Other's hunt teams.   Both action he said would distinguish this team as a special team.

A few suns later, Taelo advised that they had reached the lake suggested by Broken Spear to be the site of their hunt.

Little Otter suggested that they hunt in two teams. He designated Taelo and Golden Hawk to lead the hunt teams. He assigned Burley Bear to be on Taelo's team and he would be on Golden Hawk's team.

He pointed to a tree about fifty spear lengths away and said that the women would be assigned to the two teams based on the order that they finished the race.

The race was ready to begin, Quiet Rabbit knew she was among the fastest of the women but knew that Talking Wren often beat her. When the race started, she was surprised that Busy Bee was running as fast as she was.

She was determined to win.

She was determined to hunt with Taelo.

She put that vision in her head, her feet flew, and she pulled ahead. She was several spear lengths in front of Busy Bee as she crossed the finish line.

She knew that she would hunt with Taelo and that eventually she would fulfill Broken Spear's prediction of being Taelo's mate. It was she decided the will of the Ancestors and of her mother and father.

She did not know it at the time, but each one of the women ended up hunting with their eventual mates.

She took note that Busy Bee had made it in second and was on Golden Hawk's hunt team. She knew he was Busy Bee's target mate.

She also knew that Talking Wren had seemed to run slower than normal.   She was a good friend.

****

The long hunt teams all had good success, but Little Otter's long hunt team doubled the combined meat production of all the other long hunt teams put together.

Quiet Rabbit learned from Little Otter on his return from delivering the first load of meat to the Clan that all long hunt teams were doing well, but he proudly boasted that their team doubled the combined meat production of all the other long hunt teams.

He also shared that he had been praised for his great leadership.   But that he had made the point that the women on the team were the key factor in their hunting success.

Quiet Rabbit cut off a piece of the buffalo hump that was roasting on the spit and presented it to Little Otter with a thank you.

Talking Wren was at his side and her influence over his behavior was clear to Quiet Rabbit and Busy Bee.

Quiet Rabbit and Busy Bee later shared with White Swan, Quiet Pheasant and Floating Cloud that they had each hunted with the teams and had learned to place the spear into the chest of the buffalo from their hunt partners.

White Swan congratulated them and then shared that she had taught this hunting technique to Grey Fox Running and Fast Skimmer.   Red Oak though an excellent hunter was not fast enough to use this hunting technique.   This hunting technique was passed to her by her father.

She was sure that Fast Skimmer would have loved to have taught Quiet Rabbit, but White Swan said she was happy that Taelo had done so.

With tears of happiness, Quiet Rabbit went out to her boulder by the edge of the water.

She was sure she and Taelo would walk, they would talk, they would hold hands the way her parents had done.   She knew she and Taelo would have what her parents shared with one another.

She smiled and looked out into the harbor and thanked both for having been the parents they had been.

The End

91

<u>Busy Bee</u>

Busy Bee had rightfully earned her second name. She was always hyperactive. From little on she was a bundle of energy. Good things happened when she was properly guided and trained.

Catastrophes also happened.

She single-handedly had caused the collapse of the main meeting lodge when she had tripped over the support lines holding up the walls and had removed them.

The lodge did not fall until the leadership team was inside. Someone bumped one of the support poles and the entire structure collapsed.

Busy Bee admitted to the removal of the support lines. She was only six full seasons old. When she explained why she had done it everyone had a good laugh.

Silver Hawk commented that she had been a Busy Bee. The second name was immediately accepted by everyone.

It had an impact.

Busy Bee did not change her active behavior, but she paid much closer attention to the world around her. She now sought to understand the world before acting.

She was the daughter of Brave Deer one of the lead hunters for the Elk Clan. She became aware that his status gave her many privileges.

Her mother, Little Pebble, became her guide. Busy Bee struggled with the role the women had in the life of the clan. She spent much of her time running and playing with the boys.

She had only one friend. This friend talked her ear off. Her friend eventually earned the name Talking Wren.

Busy Bee immediately reinforced this so appropriate name.

The summer had been a wonderful time. The clan had spent the season in a new valley. It had been much farther to the east than their previous camps in the seasons before

Silent Hawk had been seeking a better hunting ground for the Elk Clan. Busy Bee did not notice the fact that hunting had not produced the amount of food needed to sustain the clan. Her father had voiced his concern, but it meant little to her. She was always well fed and did not understand his concern.

The hunting season ended in a disaster that she understood. The lead hunter, father to one of her male friends, was killed by a rhinoceros. The rhino had also severely injured several other hunters who had come to the aid of their leader. She did not know how to console her friend.

It saddened her.

It was only a few sun cycles later that the Elk Clan left their summer valley and began their journey to the Elk Clan end of hunt season meeting. It was during this journey that she learned of the very dire straits the Elk Clan faced. This was a surprise to her, and she began to wonder what she could do to help the clan.

Busy Bee felt a new sense of responsibility.

She had prepared for the Elk Clan meeting. It was her first time to have a substantial variety of goods to trade. She had been planning to trade for items like new footwear or decorations and clothing for herself.

She instead focused her trading on obtaining as much dried food as she could. She was a sharp trader and always got the amount she sought. Her goods all had a high level of dried food cost attached to them. She was surprised that she had to do little bargaining. She was pleased when all her trade goods were soon gone.

She could now focus on playing with her friends.

One of friends was Quiet Rabbit from the Elk Hide Clan. She learned about her loss of both her father and mother.

She hugged Quiet Rabbit and they both cried together. Afterwards they walked quietly through the forest.

The loss of the main hunter in the Elk Clan and now the same kind of loss in the Elk Hide Clan made her worry about her father. She wondered what she would do if she lost her mother and father.

These were new thoughts and they concerned her greatly.

Not much later she learned that the person who had given her, her second name, Silent Hawk was stepping aside and had accepted Grey Fox Running as the next leader of the Elk Clan.

She and Talking Wren both cornered Quiet Rabbit to find out what she knew about the situation.

Quiet Rabbit commented that she and her Grandmother were both joining the Elk Clan. She complemented Grey Fox Running and said he and White Swan had been a friend of her mother and father. She went on to say that he would be a very good leader.

The three celebrated the fact that they would all be together. Busy Bee let the two know about her focus on trading for dry food so she and her family would not have to worry about food.

Quiet Rabbit let them know that she and her Grandmother had also loaded up on dried fish and other dried goods. They felt vulnerable because they now had no one to hunt for them.

Busy Bee wondered out loud why the three of them could not become a hunt team. She went on to say that they could learn to throw the spear and hunt the small game like rabbits and ground hogs.

The three agreed that they would start hunting every morning before the first meal.

Busy Bee asked about Taelo and Golden Hawk. She listened to Quiet Rabbit's tales of Taelo's and Golden Hawk's early years.

How they had supplied the entire clan with crayfish. How they had saved the young children from a giant mother bear. How they had killed a huge saber tooth tiger. How they had invented a new way to fish that had made the Elk Hide Clan rich in fish.

Quiet Rabbit finished by saying that both were her friends.

Busy Bee asked which one of the two Quiet Rabbit had her eyes on. She was pleased to hear that Golden Hawk was free for her to go after.

Talking Wren laughed and said that both were daydreaming. She said competition was already on the extreme.

Quiet Rabbit suggested the three of them concentrate on becoming good hunters of small game.

Busy Bee added that they might also take up fishing in the small streams as they traveled.

Talking Wren commented that hunting and fishing were activities they could successfully control.

A few sun cycles later, they were standing with all the other Elk Clan members when Grey Fox Running and Red Oak asked for each family to present the food they had.

Floating Cloud was surprised at how much dried food Quiet Rabbit had. Her pile was more than some of Elk Clan families. It was clear to her that Quiet Rabbit had traded all her goods for dry food.

Busy Bee's pile of dried food exceeded Quiet Rabbit's. Her aggressive trading had made a difference. Brave Deer took note that his daughter had used all her trade goods for food. He gave her a hug and told her how proud he was of her.

Grey Fox Running took note at the amount of dried food the two had accumulated.

He pointed to the two large piles and commented loudly to Red Oak that the dried food would make a huge difference. He wanted to give the two recognition. He knew that Quiet Rabbit had accumulated the food during the meeting of the Clans. She had come to trade for clothes but had focused on necessities.

White Swan commented to Quiet Pheasant that they should pay attention to Quiet Rabbit's new friend Busy Bee.

Busy Bee listened with interest as Grey Fox Running instructed the hunters. She heard him telling them that what they ate each day would be what they killed each day.

She learned that the dried food that had been taken was only enough for each hunter to have two meals. When she commented about this to Quiet Rabbit, she learned that her father had been a partner to Grey Fox Running and Red Oak. He had led his hunters in the same way.

Busy Bee had been watching her father. He had never told her much about the day-to-day life when he was out hunting. She wondered how he would handle hunting with Grey Fox Running and Red Oak.

Listening to the instructions to the hunters and then joining in with the rest of the Elk Clan to cheer their departure gave Busy Bee an even greater desire to show that she, Quiet Rabbit and Talking Wren could hunt as well.

She floated this idea with her two friends and felt a surge of energy when both agreed.

Busy Bee, Quiet Rabbit and Talking Wren found it harder than they thought it would be to hunt for small game.

Over the span of seven sun cycles, the three had bagged one rabbit. That rabbit had wandered into the Elk Camp and Quiet Rabbit had hit it with a thrown stone and Busy Bee whacked it with a stick.

It was clear they needed hunting lessons.

Busy Bee commented on the fact that Taelo and Golden Hawk returned with at least a dozen rabbits each sun cycle.

Quiet Rabbit said that each sun cycle there were always two rabbits at her grandmother's cook fire.

She thought it was left by Taelo, but they had never been able to catch him in the act of leaving the rabbits.

She suggested they get hunting lessons from Taelo and Golden Hawk.

Taelo and Golden Hawk returned from their patrol around the Elk Clan's travel path with the news having found a large honeybee hive.

Busy Bee reacted with enthusiasm when the Clan stopped to gather in the honey. She had not been able to trade away two handfuls of bag containers. Now she gave one to White Swan, one to Quiet Pheasant, two to her mother, and traded four for some new boots and gloves.

She kept three. One full bag of honey would be more than each of them could eat until next hunting season.

She commented that the honey tree was an omen of good things to come.

A few sun cycles later and with no improvement in their hunting ability, Busy Bee again brought up the fact that they needed to learn to hunt better.

She wondered how they would get Taelo and Golden Hawk to teach them to hunt.

Quiet Rabbit excused herself. She walked across to where Taelo and Golden Hawk were eating.

She explained the desire of learning to hunt small game as well as he and Golden Hawk.

When Quiet Rabbit came back and let her friends know that they would get hunting lessons at the end of the coming sun cycle, Busy Bee commented that Quiet Rabbit had strengthened their bond of friendship by demonstrating that she really was friends with the two young hunters.

Talking Wren rolled her eyes and asked if there was anything useful in Busy Bee's mind.

Quiet Rabbit laughed and said that on the following sun cycle they were to meet Golden Hawk and Taelo at the edge of the camp. They would be given some hunting lessons.

Busy Bee was surprised when on meeting the two for the hunting lessons, Golden Hawk gave each of them a bag full of thumb sized stones and a new leather sling.

She wanted to dance and sing but kept her composure.

Taelo showed them the technique of loading the sling, spinning it, and then letting the sling open at the exact moment the sling reached its farthest point going forward.

He demonstrated letting the sling open early. This gave it the farthest trajectory. He demonstrated the effect on the range by letting the sling open later and slightly past the horizontal position.

Golden Hawk stepped up and gave some pointers on aiming to the right and left.

Busy Bee realized that Talking Wren seemed to have the longest range. Quiet Rabbit had the best aim. She on the other hand seemed to be a sling klutz

The lessons ended much too soon for her, but she was pleased that there would be another lesson in seven sun cycles or after each of the three killed their first small game.

She watched, as on the next sun cycle, Quiet Rabbit was the first to kill a rabbit. She and Talking Wren each had multiple opportunities to get a rabbit but missed their targets.

She complimented Quiet Rabbit but bemoaned the outcome at the end of the first sun cycle.

Three sun cycles later she finally hit her target and proudly held up the rabbit.

It was Talking Wren's lucky day. She targeted a fat ground hog that had made the mistake of coming out of his hibernation and out into the cold of winter. Talking Wren boasted that she had bagged more meat than her two competitors.

That sunset, Busy Bee sent Quiet Rabbit over to let Taelo and Golden Hawk know about their success.

She was pleased to learn that they had another hunting lesson on the following sunset.

Late in the on the following sun cycle Busy Bee looked up into the sky when an eagle let out a long cry. She did not think much about it until she heard White Swan telling Silent Hawk that the Clan should make camp. White Swan was sure that Taelo and Golden Hawk were experiencing something important.

Busy Bee asked Quiet Rabbit about the eagle's cry and learned that Quiet Rabbit also believed that Taelo and Golden Hawk would be experiencing some challenge.

She recalled the time that Taelo had faced a huge bear in a blue berry patch, while Golden Hawk led the children out of the blueberry patch to safety.

An eagle had let out a cry just before that happened.

As the sun set, Busy Bee commented that they would not get the hunting practice that they had talked about. She was now worried about her two hunting teachers.

When the eagle again let out a cry from the sky, she asked Quiet Rabbit what that meant. Quiet Rabbits response was that she was not sure but whatever Taelo and Golden Hawk had faced and experienced was over.

Busy Bee, Quiet Rabbit and Talking Wren sat with their backs to the fire ring. They were looking out into the dark of a winter night. She listened as Talking Wren quietly pointed out patterns of animals and other figures in the black star filled sky.

Then Quiet Rabbit pointed out something moving along the trail. Busy Bee jumped up and followed White Swan who had started down the trail followed by Quiet Pheasant and Floating Cloud.

She, Quiet Rabbit, Talking Wren and Floating Cloud took over pulling the heavily loaded travois. It was all the four could do to get the travois to the edge of the camp.

They readily let some of the other members of the clan take over and pull the travois the rest of the way to where White Swan had her camp.

The three helped Floating Cloud lift the dire wolf hides from the sled and stretch them on a large frame.

Together the four of them scraped the two hides and rubbed bear fat on to condition it.

They had a steady stream of old hunters and the older women come by and comment about the huge size of the wolves.

Busy Bee now was even more determined to get hunting lessons from the two.

She decided that she would help Floating Cloud make the wolf skin clothes for Taelo and Golden Hawk that they talked about making.

The next morning, she noticed that Quiet Rabbit and Floating Cloud were holding a piece of the elk meat.

She walked over to learn what they were saying and learned that Floating Cloud had just verified that Taelo had been leaving two rabbits on her fire ring on every sun cycle since the loss of Quiet Rabbit's parents.

Floating Cloud conjectured that he had left the elk meat because he did not have any rabbits to leave.

Busy Bee looked at Quiet Rabbit and smiled and gave her a hug, "you really do have good friends."

She was now more interested in Golden Hawk than ever before.

She listened to Floating Cloud's instructions on how to make a vest from the dire wolf skin. She looked over at Quiet Rabbit who was working on a similar vest.

She was listening to Talking Wren who had joined them. She wondered if Talking Wren talked in her sleep.

She was surprised when her mother joined them to help. She watched as Floating Cloud and her mother chatted and each worked on a footwear made of a mix of buffalo hide and lined the inside with rabbit fur.

When Floating Cloud made a comment about all the rabbit fur she had accumulated from Taelo's daily gift of two rabbits and how appropriate it was to give him some of it back, Busy Bee made the observation that he had his eye on Quiet Rabbit.

Quiet Rabbit looked up with a smile but did not say a word.

A few sun cycles later Busy Bee and the other four seamstresses proudly stared at two complete outfits.

The pants went from ankle to lower chest, a rabbit fur lined vest provided warmth and an outer long jacket down to mid-thigh provided another layer of protection.

The footwear was a work of art with rabbit fur lining, buffalo hide bottom and a top layer of wolf hide to make them match the pants.

She joined the rest of them in commenting at how good the two would look in this outfit.

Two sun cycles later she, Quiet Rabbit and Talking Wren stood looking out at the endless sea.

She was surprised when Floating Cloud offered Taelo and Golden Hawk dry outfits to replace their froze clothes. She had not noticed the frozen pants that they both were wearing. She and Quiet Rabbit unpacked the new outfits and gave them to Floating Cloud.

She, Quiet Rabbit and Talking Wren heard White Swan's compliment on the look of the outfits and the speed with which the outfits had been made.

She was happy to hear Floating Cloud credit everyone that had contributed.

She made a comment to Quiet Rabbit about how handsome the two looked in their new outfits.

Not long after they had put on their new outfits, Busy Bee watched as Taelo and Golden Hawk followed White Swan and Quiet Pheasant down the coast to look for a winter camp location for the Elk Clan.

She listened as Quiet Rabbit commented that she expected White Swan to find the place where the Elk Clan would spend the winter.

She was not surprised to see White Swan return first.

Then when White Swan insisted the Clan follow her to the Elk Clan's winter location, she joined Quiet Rabbit and Floating Cloud as they followed White Swan.

She felt a warm feeling when her mother took her hand and gave it a squeeze. They walked together holding hands until they reached the wonderful beach side camp location.

She joined her two friends as they took in the high spit going out to sea. It appeared that the beach had an arm held over its head to defend itself. There was even a huge boulder on the shore that was the head.

She was impressed by White Swan's guidance in getting everyone to build the central lodge structure. She eagerly joined the work.

Busy Bee noted how White Swan listened to the older hunters and then had them leading the work.   She saw how effective this was in getting everyone involved.

The lodge was almost up by the time Silent Hawk returned from his search for a winter camp.

His praise to all the Elk Clan members and his recognition of White Swan, inspired Busy Bee.   She wanted to be more like White Swan.

When Red Oak returned with his hunters, Busy Bee began to worry about her father.   He was to have returned first.

She talked with her mother and was surprised at her mother's strong conviction that her mate was alright and would return soon.

She sat with Quiet Rabbit as they listened to White Swan, Quiet Pheasant and Floating Cloud discuss the situation about the Clan of Others that had attacked Red Oak and his hunters.

It was clear to her that White Swan and Quiet Pheasant had decided on the action they planned to take.   It was also clear that the two very carefully planned their actions, chose their timing, and then manipulated the leadership.   They did not argue but set up the situation, so their proposal seemed the most logical.

She, Quiet Rabbit and Talking Wren discussed this behavior and decided they were learning an important lesson on how to be a woman in a man's environment.

She was both happy and in tears when two sun cycles later her father returned with his long hunt team.

Her tears were because her father was very badly injured. His hunt team had been hunted by a pack of vicious and aggressive dire wolves.

She knew that she had almost lost her father like Quiet Rabbit had lost hers.

She was so happy to give him a hug and that her mother had been right about him returning.

A few sun cycles later she stood with Quiet Rabbit as they watched White Swan, Quiet Pheasant, Golden Hawk and Taelo going up the coast to meet the Clan of Others.

She took note that Taelo and Golden Hawk were not wearing their dire wolf outfits but were in their normal outfits. She shared this observation with Quiet Rabbit and learned that the two considered their new wolf outfits as formal outfits to be worn on special occasions.

A handful of sun cycles later she stood next to Quiet Rabbit as they saw White Swan and Quiet Pheasant jogging toward them along the water's edge.

Both she and Quiet Rabbit let out a breath they had inadvertently held when Floating Cloud commented that even though Taelo and Golden Hawk were not present, everything was alright.

Later she listened to White Swan explain what had happened at the Clan of Others' camp.

It did not surprise her that Taelo had acted to protect White Swan. Nor did it surprise her that Golden Hawk had been ready to fight the rest of the Clan of Others.

It was a surprise to learn that the Clan of Others had been waiting for Taelo and that an eagle's cry had been the signal that connected him to the Clan of Others.

The night Grey Fox Running returned at the same time as Taelo, and Golden Hawk returned was her next big surprise.

The surprise was the escort for Taelo and Golden Hawk. Busy Bee noted the huge person introduced by Grey Fox Running as Burley Bear. He was larger than Little Otter, the largest person she had ever seen.

She, Quiet Rabbit and Talking Wren discussed Taelo's status among the clan of Others and that they had sent four of their warriors to protect him.

They decided that there was something special about Taelo. She agreed with Talking Wren when she voiced that whoever he chose as a mate would be a very lucky person.

One moon cycle later she learned that Taelo and Golden Hawk had left the camp.

She watched as Burley Bear climbed the cliff behind the camp. He was carrying a pack on his back that was almost the same size as himself. She wondered how he had the strength to pull himself up. It was clear to her that he was stronger than anyone in the Elk Clan.

She, Quiet Rabbit and Talking Wren spent every sunset discussing what the three might be doing and how they were faring.

Three moon cycles later she was standing at the top of the cove spit cliff next to Quiet Rabbit as they looked at three figures coming up the coast.

She easily picked out Burley Bear. He was the giant in the middle between two seemingly small figures. The three were pulling a huge load behind them.

Grey Fox Running announced that their wayward young men had returned.

She and a host of other Elk Clan members rushed out to meet them. The huge load turned out to be the meat of three buffalo. It was meat that the clan badly needed.

Busy Bee took note that the return of the three signaled the beginning of a period of good fortune for the entire Elk Clan.

She was relieved at their return and the news of a huge herd of buffalo that resided in a valley not far from the clan.

Then Taelo announced that he, Golden Hawk and Burley Bear were planning to build a fish trap in the small harbor in front of the camp.

Busy Bee discussed this with Quiet Rabbit and Talking Wren.

It was then that she learned of Talking Wren's skill at organizing people and getting work done. She was impressed with her friend's logical thinking. She talked a lot, but she also thought a lot.

She watched Talking Wren organize the logistics of gathering the required materials needed to build the huge fish trap.

She did whatever was asked of her. She was content leading and doing what Taelo requested and what Talking Wren organized. She watched Quiet Rabbit skillfully coach the younger members of the clan.

The opening of the fish trap caught some Elk Clan members off guard. The fish processing area could barely keep up with the quantity of fish being brought to them.

Busy Bee noted that the members of the Clan of Others that had been invited for the opening of the fish trap were processing more fish than the Elk Clan members.

The Others worked steadily and were very fast at cleaning the fish. It was clear their strength made the work of processing the large fish easier.

Spring found Busy Bee going along the sea going spit cliffs collecting bird eggs. She and Quiet Rabbit had agreed that they would only take one egg from each nest. They had felt guilty taking the eggs from the mother and decided they would always leave one egg. Talking Wren laughed at their sentiment but agreed to follow their lead.

Some eggs were eaten fresh, but most were boiled and then arranged in layers separated by grass and put in a cool area.

The three also tended a salt making area at the foot of the spit. This was an area selected by Floating Cloud. It produced more salt than Busy Bee had ever seen in her lifetime.

She commented that she, Quiet Rabbit and Talking Wren would have so much salt that they would be among those considered very well to do. She had no doubt that she and her friends were some of the hardest workers in the clan.

When Taelo, Golden Hawk and Burley Bear killed the largest shark she had ever seen and then gave her, Quiet Rabbit and Talking Wren public recognition for making the fish trap possible and awarded three of the largest shark teeth and a handful of additional teeth to each of them, she knew she was hooked on all three of them.

She commented to Quiet Rabbit and Talking Wren how special she thought they were.

Quiet Rabbit smiled and nodded but said nothing.

Busy Bee enjoyed the season. It seemed to her to flow a smooth warm quiet river. She worked hard in the morning processing the salt from the salt flat. Then she, Quiet Rabbit and Talking Wren would take a swim and then lay on the top of the huge boulder they called Head Rock.

They would watch Taelo, Golden Hawk and Burley Bear tend to the salt flat the three had established. It was clear to her that the three would be three young hunters with the most to trade when it came to the Elk Clan meeting.

She commented on the amount of fish and other sea food that the three were accumulating. Quiet Rabbit commented that every sunrise Floating Cloud found a fish and a small bag of salt at their fire ring. She was sure the three would be as generous at the coming Elk Clan meeting as they were at the seaside camp.

The cool air signaled, to Busy Bee and her two close friends, the arrival of the coming winter. The swimming stopped but mining their salt flat and sitting at the top of Head Rock and talking continued.

She knew they had become fast friends.

She knew the hunters were preparing to for their seasonal long hunt. Her father had recovered and only had a few scars from the previous year's battle with the dire wolves.

She, Quiet Rabbit and Talking Wren watched as White Swan, Quiet Pheasant and Floating Cloud walked up the slope to where the three were sitting at the top of the Head Rock.

She almost fell off the boulder she was sitting on when Quiet Pheasant suggested the three of them plan on going on a long hunt.

White Swan explained she had arranged for a mixed gender hunt team to participate in this hunt season. Grey Fox Running was arranging the makeup of the team and getting agreement to it at the very moment.

Busy Bee looked at her two friends and knew immediately that they were all eager to go on a long hunt.

She listened as Quiet Rabbit asked who was on the team.

It was hard to keep from shouting as she heart that Taelo, Golden Hawk and Burley Bear were three of the hunters.

The fourth was being debated. A few of the leadership objected to the mixed gender makeup of the team. They wanted someone in charge that they felt would be on their side.

They named Little Otter as the leader.

All three almost simultaneously blurted out, "You must be kidding."

Busy Bee listened to her father's instructions. It was easy for her to agree to his message to trust Taelo and Golden Hawk and listen to their hunting advice.

She, Quiet Rabbit and Talking Wren prepared for everything they could think of. They had become proficient in the use of their sling and knew they would not go hungry.

Quiet Rabbit went one step farther and asked Taelo and Golden Hawk for their advice of what should be part of the goods to take on a long hunt.

Taelo, Golden Hawk met them at the top of the Head Rock. They showed each item they were planning to carry.

Then the two presented a spear to each of the three. Each spear had a symbol carved into it. Busy Bee had a honeybee carved into the shaft. Quiet Rabbit had a small rabbit carved into the same area. Talking Wren had a small wren carved into the same area.

Busy Bee laughed when she saw that the small wren had music floating up the shaft.

The long hunt teams were sent off a few sun cycles after the meeting at the top of Head Rock.

She was surprised when their team went up the coast. Burley Bear shared that he needed to get his hunting gear.

All three of them knew that he had everything he need.

They arrived at the cave of the Clan of the Others after spending a night at the place where Taelo had first met Burley Bear. The next sun cycle they passed the beach where Taelo had found the whale.

She thought it appropriate that it was now referred to as Whale's Beach.

As the sun was reaching the far edge of the sea, she saw the entire Clan of Others out on the beach to greet Taelo.

It was very clear to Busy Bee that Taelo was a hero figure to the Others.

She, Quiet Rabbit and Talking Wren all took in a deep breath of amazement when they followed Taelo and a badly disfigured person into the Cave of the Others. The first thing they noticed was the steaming pool and the water raining down from above.

Then they caught their breath as they took in the view of the broad valley beyond that appeared to have two hands formed by the mountains holding a lush forest and a small river running down its middle.

All three had stopped with their mouth open. Busy Bee commented that she thought she was at the entrance to paradise.

Then they stripped off their outer clothing and followed Taelo and the person she learned was the Seer as they entered the hot water pool and let the shower drench them.

Little Otter joined them as they sat on strategically placed boulders.

Busy Bee let out a moan of pleasure and commented that they would need to visit the Others as often as possible.

The celebration featuring an evening meal and an almost all-night story telling session drove home how important Taelo was to the Others.

Busy Bee was exhausted by the time she finally crawled under her sleeping hide and closed her eyes.

The next morning, She and the rest of the team listened to Broken Spear, the Seer. He commented that an additional hunter would be added to the team. Meadow Flower, Burley Bear's, mate to be, would be joining them.

He went on to say that in this way Burley bear would have his mate along and match the makeup of the team.

Busy Bee almost fell of the boulder she was sitting on. She looked over at Quiet Rabbit and watched a small smile cross her friends face.

The team left a sun cycle later and headed to a new hunting ground that had been offered by Quiet Fox, Burley Bear's father and the leader of the Others.

Busy Bee jokingly commented that she now understood Burley Bear's need to visit his clan to get his hunting weapon. She said she recognized Meadow Flower as a powerful weapon.

Busy Bee thought the location Taelo chose to make their hunting camp was perfect. She was at first skeptical about the need to make her sleeping location up in the limbs of the giant tree that dominated the camp.

When she heard Taelo describe the animals that might attack them she was eager to get her location put up.

Then came the moment when Little Otter explained how the hunt team would be set up. She listened as he explained that the fastest person would accompany Taelo. The second fastest would accompany Golden Hawk. The third fastest would be with Burley Bear and the slowest would be matched with him.

Busy Bee believed she could outrun any of her friends and certainly she was going to be faster than Meadow Flower

The race started when Little Otter dropped the stone he held in his hand. The race was to a tree a good three spear throws away. She was going full out and was first to the tree.

She was surprised when she was passed by Quiet Rabbit. She tried to catch up, but it was clear that the gap was growing.

She knew that Quiet Rabbit would be hunting with Taelo.

Busy Bee looked over her shoulders into the eyes of Talking Wren. The wink from her friend seemed to be the energy she needed to find the extra boost to cross the finish in the second position.

She would hunt with Golden Hawk.

She was exhausted as she listened to Little Otter arrange the teams.

She was surprised to hear Little Otter say that he was changing the pairing of Talking Wren and Meadow Flower. He explained that it would be essential to clearly understand each other during the hunt.

Since he did not know the language of the Others, he was pairing Meadow Flower and Burley Bear and they would be supporting Taelo. He and Talking Wren would be supporting Golden Hawk.

She pulled all the women together and gave them a group hug.

She was where she wanted to be and hunting with the person she wanted to be with.

The End

<u>Little Otter & Talking Wren</u>

alking Wren had informed her parents of her desire to be part of the long hunt team. They at first questioned her desire but they knew that her two friends had chosen to be on the hunt team. Talking Wren listened as each of her parents gave their version of approval.

Her mother focused on being careful and being safe.

Her father spent time with giving her hunting tips and showing her how to use a spear.

He was Impressed when she showed him the spear made by Taelo, Golden Hawk and Burley Bear. He commented on both its good balance, the quality of the wood and its beauty. He said that such attention to detail and the fact that the three were looking out for her was a good sign.

His comments seemed to help her mother accept the hunting arrangement. Her mother gave her a large sleeping hide and a soft covering hide to keep her warm.

Talking Wren knew that it was her way of saying she thought it would be a great opportunity for her daughter.

She knew immediately that it was going to be a good long hunt when Taelo suggested to Little Otter that Burley Bear lead the way to the Cave of the Other because he had to pick up a few critical hunting items.

She suspected that a change from the crappy hunting ground area they had been assigned was going to happen.

The cave of the Others impressed and overwhelmed Talking Wren. It was massive, spacious, and blessed with an amazing panoramic view.

Her mind immediately began to analyze the layout and the well-organized arrangement of the living quarters and the gathering area. She went to the warm water pool and dipped her hand in. She stood looking out at the long-lush valley beyond the pool. It was clear to her that the Others had a home that would be wanted by everyone. She envied the clans good fortune.

She had heard the story of how Taelo had found the cave and it came to her as she turned slowly around to take it all in.

He had been led to it by a large male elk.

The eagle had cried out from above.

She wished the animals talked to her as they did to Taelo.

She thought about the hard winter they had just lived through and imagined what it would have been like if every day she could have bathed in the warm water pool. She envied the luxury enjoyed by the Others.

No wonder the entire clan had been out on the beach to greet Taelo.

She saw Taelo and the person she had learned was Broken Spear, the Seer of the Others lead the way into the pool, she followed the rest of the team and sat down on boulders that had been placed beneath the water.

The water was up to her shoulders. She closed her eyes and let the heat warm her.

Later, after the team set up their sleeping area, she was seated on a convenient boulder and eating a very well-prepared buffalo meat dinner that was flavored in an unusual but very tasty way. She was listening to Taelo, Golden Hawk and Broken Spear discuss the upcoming hunt.

She was caught by surprise when Broken Spear commented about having Meadow Flower, Burley Bear's future mate, join the long hunt team so that he would not be the only one that was not paired with a future mate.

Meadow Flower looked at each of the male Elk Clan members. Taelo and Golden Hawk were already the target of her two friends, Quiet Rabbit and Busy Bee.

That left Little Otter for her.

She had long ago decided that his name was misleading. He was a large powerful person at least three times her size.

She wondered whether the Seer was mistaken in his assessment of the team.

She almost fell off her boulder, when Broken Spear looked over at her and gave her a wink and a nod.

She found it hard to swallow when he went on to comment that the long hunt experience would bond them all for life.

She looked again at Little Otter. She decided that he was very large, but he was just as handsome as Taelo or Golden Hawk. She would see if he had other redeeming qualities.

This was a situation that she had not imagined.

Little Otter had taken in the discussion and wondered which of the three women on the hunt team was the one meant for him. He was confident in himself but extremely shy and had not even thought about hunting with a potential mate.

The discussion disturbed him, and he decided that he would let the leaves blow as they may.

He knew he had been selected to lead the long hunt only because a few of the leaders objected to Taelo or Golden Hawk as the leaders.

The objection was actually about having women on the hunt team, but the objectors did not want to challenge Taelo's mother, White Swan. They had come to recognize that she was astute at managing the politics of the Elk Clan.

Little Otter was pleased to have been the third person selected. He had not expected to have been considered to hunt with the likes of the other three male hunters on the team. He had observed their capabilities and knew his hunting skills were a distant fourth behind.

As they left the Clan of Others and Burley Bear led the team in a new direction, Little Otter realized he was in charge in name only. He had no idea where they would hunt. He wondered if he had lost his leadership position.

Taelo, Golden Hawk and Burley Bear had agreed to hunt in a more abundant location than the desert area originally designated to the team.

They had agreed to give one third of their take to the Clan of Others and to share all the buffalo that the Others could hunt from the Valley of Plenty.

Little Otter was pleased to be hunting in a more promising region. He had not especially liked the attitude of the leaders that had told him that little was expected of his team and he should just concentrate in keeping the women safe.

When they arrived at the site suggested by Broken Spear, Taelo announced that Little Otter should organize the team and prepare for the hunt.

He was pleased that Taelo was not taking over the leadership role. He stepped forward and announced that teams would be organized based on the speed of each member.

He stated that he knew Taelo, and Golden Hawk were the two fastest. They would each lead a hunt team.

He had no idea about the women and had decided on a race to see how to place each of them. He explained that the fastest would be placed with Taelo, the second fastest with Golden Hawk, the third fastest with Burley Bear and the slowest with him.

The outcome was very clear. Quiet Rabbit seemed to fly past all the others. Busy Bee was a distant second just ahead of Talking Wren who seemed not be trying to beat her two friends.

He knew Meadow Flower, would be last. The Others were powerful but not built for speed.

He had planned to put the third fastest woman with Burley Bear. He figured it would be Talking Wren.

Taelo, had casually commented that clear communication between partners was very important.

He was not fluent in the language of the Others and knew that Meadow Flower had limited understanding of his language.

This caused him to change Meadow Flower from supporting Golden Hawk to pairing her with Burley Bear.

He reassigned Talking Wren to be his hunt partner.

Talking Wren thought back through the race. When the race had started, she had taken the lead and stayed in front out to the marker tree.

As she went around it, she was passed by Busy Bee.

Then Quiet Rabbit surprised her by passing them both and stretching her lead by at least three spears lengths.

It was clear to her that Quiet Rabbit had dug deep for all the speed she could muster.

She had thought about passing Busy Bee but decided against it because she realized that Busy Bee wanted to hunt with Golden Hawk.

She relaxed and took third.

The outcome was very clear.

She was surprised when Little Otter changed the hunt pair assignments. His logic about needing clear communication between hunt partners made sense and she readily accepted working with him.

The hunt began immediately after having been paired. She and Little Otter followed Golden Hawk and Busy Bee. They listened to his hunt instructions to Busy Bee.

She quickly realized that Busy Bee would need to carry two spears and keep up with Golden Hawk as he raced forward carrying an additional two spears.

He said that he was targeting four buffalo.

Talking Wren clearly understood that Golden Hawk was planning on at least three buffalo with a fourth one if he was fast enough.

She commented that she and Little Otter would do their part.

Talking Wren turned to Little Otter and asked if downing four buffalo as described by Golden Hawk was possible?

Little Otter replied that he thought Golden Hawk was exaggerating and that if they got one buffalo between the two teams, they would be lucky.

Golden Hawk dropped back and joined the two as they jogged out toward the herd. He explained how the two should ensure each animal was dead and then gut them and prepare them to be hauled into the forest where they would be hung up and processed.

She then remembered Burley Bear's story about watching Taelo and Golden Hawk take down the three buffalo they had brought back on the sled that pulled to the Elk Clan.

Then the hunt began.

Talking Wren was impressed at Golden Hawk's ability to cull out four young buffalo and get them moving toward the forest. When Golden Hawk began the run, she and Little Otter followed as closely as possible, but they could not keep up.

She kept looking ahead as the first two buffalo dropped to their knees. They were dead.

Golden Hawk did not stop.

She watched as Busy Bee sped up to hand him the next spear.

He ran out ahead and downed the third buffalo.

She wondered how Busy Bee had been able to keep up as she hand Golden Hawk the fourth spear.

What blew her mind was Golden Hawk's ability to accelerate, pass and plant the spear for the fourth buffalo to skewer itself.

She thought he had been running at top speed. Then, he left Busy Bee behind and pulled ahead of the fourth buffalo and plant the spear.

She and Little Otter found each buffalo dead and in the same front kneeling position with a spear deeply imbedded between its front legs.

She was sure each spear had gone through the heart.

She looked back to where Taelo's team had hunted and saw them pulling a buffalo into the woods. She wondered how many buffalo they had taken down.

She thought of renaming him Talking Otter as she listened to Little Otter go on and on about his team killing four buffalo. He urged Taelo and his team to help Golden Hawk and his team. "After all they had killed four ..four buffalo."

She watched as Taelo and Burly Bear pulled one of their team's kill into the woods.

Later, by her count she realized that Taelo's team had also killed four and were processing their last buffalo. She wondered how they could have done it so fast.

Her team was still processing their second one.

As she watched Burley Bear and Meadow flower and how fast they were at skinning their last animal she understood how Taelo's team had been so fast to hang their kill. She and Little Otter were snails in comparison to them.

She watched as Taelo and Quiet Rabbit went out to the herd. She did not get a satisfying answer from Burley Bear when she asked what Taelo was doing.

He said something about an out of season young calf.

She joined the other members of the team as they stood at the edge of the forest to see what Taelo was up to. She realized how good he was at staying out of sight. She could see the mother buffalo slowly move away from the main herd and come towards the woods, but she could not see either Taelo or Quiet Rabbit.

Taelo was much closer to the Buffalo than Talking Wren expected. His take down of the rather large calf was swift and effective.

Then Talking Wren drew a deep breath as Quite Rabbit jumped up to block the mother buffalo. She could not help but yell encouragement to her friend. She was pleased that the rest of the team joined her on her second yell.

Meadow Flower commented that they did not have to worry about Quiet Rabbit. Quiet Rabbit had repeatedly demonstrated her bravery and now she was armed with yet another skill.

Had the mother buffalo charged Quiet Rabbit would have used that skill to plant the spear and kill her.

By late afternoon, Talking Wren walked alongside the travois being pulled by the young but large buffalo. The travois was loaded with an entire buffalo carcass.

This was a very strange experience. She was not sure how to take it in.

She asked Taelo several times how he had figured out that the young bull would pull the travois.

Taelo's response had been that the memory of he, Golden Hawk and Burly Bear pulling the sled with three buffalo from the valley of plenty and up the beach to the Elk Clan's camp had inspired him to think about getting someone or something else to pull the travois.

He jokingly commented that it was either the bull or the three women on the team that he had chosen for the chore.

He said he had been so afraid of the second choice that he had taken the huge risk with the young bull.

The power of the young buffalo gave Talking Wren a lesson in applying one's observation and to extend that learning to something beyond what she knew.

She likened it to Taelo extrapolating a small river fish catching trap to an extremely large one that fit the scale of the cove and the ocean.

She was aware that Taelo had come up with the fish trap by watching how a group of adults guided the spent salmon to the edge of the river before picking them up and taking them to shore.

Now he had thought through the act of pulling the heavy sled and extended this to having an animal do it.

She commented that he had been wise to choose the young buffalo to pull the travois.

He smiled at her and said that the young bull had been sent to him by the Ancestors who had communicated the same sentiment that he should choose wisely.

He said he had taken the easier path with the young bull.

She promised herself that she would figure out how to do something similar.

When Little Otter volunteered to take the first load of meat to the Clan of the Others and then onto the Elk Clan, she volunteered to be his travel partner.

She would have preferred to have stayed to hunt with the rest of the team but chose to support her hunt partner.

She figured it might give them some time to learn more about each other.

She was surprised at the speed and distance they could travel during each sun cycle. Had they been pulling the heavy load they would have been exhausted after each sun cycle. Instead, they were able to enjoy a well-cooked evening meal.

The nights were getting increasingly colder, and she found that sleeping next to Little Otter was like sleeping next to a warming fire.

She smiled as she thought about such an arrangement.

He was a good listener and gave her complements on everything she prepared on the cooking fire.

He was also a much deeper thinker than she had given him credit. He was constantly posing questions that required her to stop and think before replying.

His questions seemed to open knew thought paths for her.

Talking Wren gained a deeper understanding of her hunt partner and became less concerned about Broken Spear's prediction of mates hunting together.

Broken Spear's and the Clan of Others' greetings, and a welcome dinner put Talking Wren at ease.

She talked with Broken Spear as they ate dinner.

She listened carefully as he explained that Taelo would face a life-threatening experience while she and Little Otter were away.

The journey down the coast toward the Elk Clan cove was serene. The coastal wind was at their back and the sun was to their front.

Little Otter and the young buffalo seemed to have formed a strong and smooth working relationship. Their steady pace took them to their destination in just three sun cycles.

Talking Wren kept her feet dry, but she walked along the edge of the sea and collected any unique seashell or other objects that she could later use to decorate the clothes she would make. Occasionally she would find a unique object that she would use to make something unique.

Little Otter found the young buffalo comforting. It seemed to have bonded with him and responded positively to being brushed and occasionally fed grasses and some ground roots.

He listened to Talking Wren's chatter and found it interesting as she went from the analysis of the wind's interaction with the waves, to the reason the moon's appearance changed throughout the seasons, to how she would use some found object to decorate a jacket she planned to make. It was clear to him that her mind was moving about in an almost random fashion trying to analyze the world around her.

He was impressed with the range of thoughts that seemed to flow unstopped from brain to tongue and out into the world.

He was pleased to learn that his team was the first to send back a significant amount of meat. He consciously avoided telling the leaders, that had sent his team to the worst hunting grounds, that his team was not hunting where they had been sent.

He instead let them know that his team's long hunt had just begun.

To his parents and to White Swan, Quiet Pheasant and Floating Cloud he shared that he was learning more than he had ever known about hunting and about what it meant to lead.

He complemented the skill and bravery of the young women on the team.

Talking Wren was impressed with Little Otter's comments and the maturity that it signified.

The trip back, with no load, went at the jogging pace they could maintain. The young bull carried all their load on its back.

During their travel, Talking Wren brought up the life-threatening experience that Taelo might have had. She wondered what that might have been.

Little Otter's practical reply that they would know when they returned to the camp site was not very satisfying, but it was irrefutable.

When she entered the camp, she was immediately drawn to a huge, stretched hide that Talking Wren learned was a saber tooth tiger. It was as large as the hide of a buffalo. She stood before it and asked how the team had killed it.

She looked at Taelo when she learned that he alone had killed it. She was not expecting an answer when she asked how that was possible. Then she went on to ask about how it had all come about.

Burley Bear stood up and told the tale of the tiger making the mistake of climbing out on the limb where Taelo was asleep. He told how Taelo had pushed the tiger off the limb and then chased after it. He held up two very long saber teeth. He went on to say that when Taelo caught up with the saber tooth tiger he attacked her and grabbed the two teeth and pulled them out as the tigress roared in pain. He then used her own teeth to kill her.

He went on to describe Taelo's egotistical, superior attitude when he had insisted the rest of the team carry the huge carcass back to camp. He then had them skin the beast and prepare the hide to make him a future victory outfit.

With a small smile he insisted that every word he had just spoken was true.

Both Talking Wren and Little Otter chuckled and then joined the rest of the team in congratulating him on his good story telling.

Talking Wren was happy to be back with the team. She then noticed that Quiet Rabbit and Meadow Flower were not in the camp.

Her inquiry about Quiet Rabbit drew out the real story of the crazed tigress and her attacks on the hunt team of the Others and then the attack on Taelo.

She was not surprised at Quiet Rabbit's bravery at chasing after the crazed tigress that was chasing Taelo.

Nor was she surprised by Quiet Rabbits ability to attend to the severe injuries of the wounded hunter.

She was well aware of her friend's quiet intensity, her focused nature and her ability to use her many skills.

She gave Little Otter a hug and commented that his sleeping area had been on the same limb as Taelo's, and the tigress passed by it on the way out to where Taelo slept.

She commented that had he been here he would have had to pull the teeth out and kill her with them because he would not have been able to run as fast or as far as Taelo.

She went on to add that she was not as brave as Quiet Rabbit and would have just yelled words of encouragement down to him from her place up in the tree.

Little Otter smiled and commented that he had thought ahead, and he had volunteered to take the meat to the two clans in the anticipation of just such an incident.

He went on to say that he had been designated as the leader for his ability to think ahead and this incident demonstrated his superior capability.

The next morning Talking Wren watched as Taelo made the stone marker that pointed the direction in which the team would move.

She asked about the drawings of a mastodon in the dirt in the direction the rocks pointed.

Taelo explained that he and Golden Hawk had spotted a large herd traveling slowly southward along the valley where they had hunted the buffalo. He wanted to keep them in sight but said he had no intentions of hunting them until Meadow Flower and Quiet Rabbit rejoined the team.

Talking Wren discussed this with Little Otter. He let her know that Taelo, Golden Hawk and Burley Bear had shared this information with him and that he was in agreement.

Talking Wren began seeing the mate she had been looking for. She also revisited all the words that Broken Spear had spoken to her. One phrase he had shared with her became central.

"You must stand behind your mate and be ready. If you do, you will have a long and prosperous time together."

She was not sure what that meant but she would stay alert and pay attention to her surroundings.

The slow movement of the mix of buffalo and Mastodons allowed the team the luxury of hunting the smaller game like elk, deer, a few boars and the smaller game like rabbits and squirrels.

Talking Wren enjoyed her time hunting with her sling. She and Busy Bee competed on how many rabbits each could bag. She noted that Busy Bee had moved from being the ham-handed slinger to a deadly accurate slinger.

She commented on the change. Busy Bee smiled and replied that she had received hands on training from an expert.

Talking Wren knew better than to pursue the meaning of that comment.

She noticed the pine tree forest thin out. The small game changed in proportion. There were fewer ground hogs and more rabbits. The terrain was covered with more protruding rocks.

She commented on this and learned that the original hunt area that had been assigned to them was farther to the east and even more sparse than the area they were now entering.

Late in the afternoon she saw two people approaching that she knew could only be Quiet Rabbit and Meadow Flower. The two made an odd pair. They were both about the same height, but she compared Quiet Rabbit to a thin willow pole and Meadow Flower to a wide strong oak.

As she called out to the rest of the team, she noted that Burley Bear was already arranging a cooking fire ring and had several cuts of meat on a skewer.

It was clear to her that he had observed the two long before she had.

The Other's had eyesight that was much better than those of the Elk Clan.

She greeted the two as they arrived and immediately reassured Quiet Rabbit that Taelo and Golden Hawk were not hunting mastodons.

She listened as Busy Bee made the point that Taelo had wanted the whole team to participate in what he was calling a once in a lifetime hunt experience that should be shared.

She watched as Taelo, Golden Hawk and Little Otter returned. Each was carrying a portion of what she thought would be a young boar.

Taelo greeted Quiet Rabbit and gave her a hug. He went on to ask how Rolling Stone was doing.

Meadow Flower replied that he was now in the good hands of her sister, Marigold. She assured the team that Marigold would give him the best care anyone could possibly get.

She also let the team know that Broken Spear had renamed Rolling Stone and he was now Saber Scar.

Everyone on the team agreed that the name was appropriate.

He would carry a set of five scars across his chest put there by the mad saber tooth tigress.

Talking Wren was amazed as she listened to Meadow Flower describe how Quiet Rabbit had cleaned the wounds and sutured the five long slashes. She had lost count of the stitches and she joked that Saber Scar now owed Quiet Rabbit a year's supply of honey for the honey Quiet Rabbit used to put in his wound.

The conversation shifted to the up-coming mammoth hunt. She was very interested and listened intently as Taelo explained how the team would hunt the Mastodon.

He explained that it was not a matter of speed, or a matter of attacking the animal.

This animal was so big that their team did not have enough members for an open terrain confrontation. The hunt was more of a trapping effort. He reminded everyone of the fish trap. The fish swam in and then could not swim out.

Talking Wren closed her eyes as she listened. It was clear to her that Taelo had figured out some way to trap the mastodon.

When Taelo described the need for a tight crevasse with sides that were wide at the opening and then narrowed as it reached its end, she immediately understood how the team would kill the animal.

At sunrise she helped clean up their campsite. She was eager to catch up to the mastodon herd.

She had watched Golden Hawk, Taelo and Quiet Rabbit as they jogged ahead to find a place where the trap could be set.

Her goal was to have the team as close to the herd as possible so they would be able to help.

Burley Bear commented that his clan had hunted the mastodon, but their technique had been to run the animal over a cliff. He said that it often resulted in killing more animals than was needed.

Talking Wren agreed that it would be difficult to control a herd of mastodon that had been driven toward a cliff.

She wondered how Taelo would be able to get one mastodon to move away from the herd and into a crevasse. She recalled his skill, when he had culled out the mother buffalo and her calf. She envisioned him doing something similar with a young mammoth.

Quiet Rabbit's return as the sun set was frustrating to Talking Wren. She had trouble sleeping, she wanted to be where the action would take place.

At sunrise she was pushing everyone to get moving. She, Quiet Rabbit and Busy Bee jogged out ahead of the rest. She knew that Quiet Rabbit was concerned that Taelo and Golden Hawk would act before the team got to where they were.

She expressed confidence that Taelo and Golden Hawk would act sensibly.

The crevasse was immediately obvious to Talking Wren. She took in the inward pointing poles. It was a fish trap extrapolated to be applied to a mastodon.

She led the way up along the top side of the crevasse to where it turned, and she could see the young mastodon trapped by the pointed poles behind him. She waved to Taelo and Golden Hawk who were sitting in front of the trapped animal.

Taelo apologized for having guided the mastodon into the crevasse before the team arrived. It had been a matter of timing of the passing herd.

He explained the preparation. He and Golden Hawk had prepared two handful of poles by burning the ends in the fire and creating the sharp points.

They had watched the herd passing by and realized that they would have to guide one mastodon at the edge of the herd toward the crevasse.

They had culled the last young mastodon and slowly moved him toward the crevasse. Once the animal was at the entrance, he and Golden Hawk had stood up waving two hides attached to long poles and yelling to get the mastodon to run into the ravine. They then planted six poles with their points very near to the mastodon's rear. Each time he back up the poles poked him, and he moved farther into the ravine.

The young mastodon that was currently trapped had just reached the end.

Taelo asked if the team was ready to send the mastodon to the land of the ancestors.

The team were eager and said so.

Talking Wren looked up in surprise as Taelo asked Burley Bear and Little Otter to be the two to drive spears into the mastodon.

She was immediately on the alert.

Broken Spears words, "you must stand behind your mate," thundered through her mind as Taelo positioned Burley Bear and then asked Meadow Flower to stand behind him.

He looked up and seemed to look at her.

A shiver ran down her spine as she immediately took a position behind Little Otter.

Taelo asked if everyone was ready.

Talking Wren took in the team. Burley Bear and Meadow Flower were directly across from Little Otter and her. Quiet Rabbit was standing next to Taelo and Busy Bee was standing next to Golden Hawk.

The sky over head was a deep blue and there was one lone cloud slowly moving toward the sun.

The cry of the eagle brought her attention to the moment.

She was grabbing for Little Otter even before he slipped on the snow-covered slope.

She had him by the hair.

She pulled him with all her might, took two steps backward and fell but held tight to Little Otter's hair.

The final part of Broken Spear message to her.

"If you do, you will have a long and prosperous time together," went through her mind as she struggled to get out from under Little Otter.

He was holding his head as she sat down beside him. He thanked her for saving his life. He knew that had he fallen into the trench he would have been trampled.

He put his arm around her and gave her a hug.

Talking Wren did not say a word. She was absorbing the fact that she had just met her lifetime mate.

High above the eagle let out a cry and flew away.

Talking Wren looked over at Taelo. He nodded his head in the same manner as Broken Spear.

She surmised that he had somehow known what was about to happen.

She looked up to the eagle that had spoken to her and knew that at the cave of the Others, Broken Spear would have watched and knew that she had listened to his words.

She spent the rest of the hunt and the travel back to the clan in a relatively quiet evaluation of her new understanding.

When Busy Bee and Quiet Rabbit asked if she was not feeling well, she laughed and replied that she was feeling better than she had ever felt.

She realized that she had drawn their attention because she had been talking a lot less.

Perhaps that was a good thing.   She was in a place she had not expected to be, but she was where she knew she wanted to be.

The End

145

Burley Bear & Meadow Flower

*T*he stand of massive, tall straight pines provided Burley Bear shade and the luxury of relaxing as he recovered from having hoisted four massive buffalo into the trees.

Meadow Flower sat next to him on the body of an ancient pine that had lost its hold on the earth. As it fell it had ripped the limbs off the younger surrounding trees. It left a streak of the blue sky to testify to the path the giant pine had taken on its way down.

He wondered how loud such a fall would have been. He took note of the breeze entering from the edge of the forest and rising past him on its way upward through the opening above. The opening provided a natural path for the wind.

He thought back to the oddity of how his current clan had come to be. It was made up of the unification of many small three and four family clans that had banded together after an especially hard and devastating winter.

Prior to that winter the various small clans had been spread out so each small clan could hunt uncontested in their territory.

This had worked for thousands of moon cycles. Then the loss of almost half of the small clan groups to an extremely cold and snow driven season had caused this practice to change.

His clan and about ten handful of other clans had come together. The combined clans moved across vast snow-covered territory and had ended making their primary camp in a green trench valley to the east of their current location.

It was during this period when their current seer, Broken Spear had earned his name. He had been mauled by a huge bear that had left him with many broken bones and a disfigured face.

He had been broken but he had been given new powers by the ancients. His new powers included flying with the birds and seeing through their eyes.

Burley Bear was just a youngster when Broken Spear had predicted that a man of the eagle would come to lead the clan to a new home. It was many moons later that he and the clan again faced a devastating winter. They were barely keeping all the families fed.

It was in the beginning of that winter when Broken Spear told the clan that they should go to the ocean shore and wait for the man of the eagle to guide them to a new home.

It was a crazy time to make such a move. Burley Bear made his voice heard but Quiet Fox his father and the leader of the clan listened to Broken Spear.

The clan moved to a perilous location by the sea.

Burley Bear's scouting led him to a camp of the New Ones that was processing a large amount of meat. Somehow the leader of the hunt group sensed his presence.

Later when he led a team to take the meat from the new ones, they tricked him by loading the travois they pulled with wood covered by a small amount of meat.

He became the laughingstock of the old hunters, and they asked him if he could tell the difference between wood and meat.

A few suns later he watched as a travois pulled by two women of the New Ones and two young boys approached the clan. They came with gifts of some small goods and more meat than he had taken from the four travois his team had captured.

He had not meant to be rude, but the strength of his grip was more than he meant it to be when he grabbed the woman with the white feather in her hair.

The next thing he remembered was awakening in his hutch. He knew immediately that an unseen warrior had blind-sided him. He came out of his hutch roaring and ready to fight.

Instead of the pandemonium and fighting that he had expected, he found Quiet Fox talking to the taller of the two young men.

As he approached the young man stood up.

At the same time an eagle let out a loud scream overhead.

There was total silence as the young man introduced himself as the claw of the eagle.

The claw of the eagle, Taelo, had defended his mother and put out his lights. He had done what no other person in the clan had ever been able to do.

He had overcome Burley Bear.

The eagle passed overhead and let out another scream.

Burley Bear took it was a signal to him. He apologized to Taelo's mother and shook Taelo's hand.

Then, another surprise, Quiet Fox asked for him to be Taelo's defender and look out for him.

In time, his relationship with Taelo and Golden Hawk became so close that he now thought of them as brothers.

After that it seemed that good things just kept happening.

Taelo led them to a whale on the beach.

Next, he found a home for the clan that included a warm water pool.

Then on a journey where the three of them moved into manhood together, they found the valley of plenty where a sea of buffalo wintered.

Then in the spring they put up a fish trap that yielded enough fish for both the Elk Clan and his clan that was referred to by the new ones as the Clan of Others.

Taelo had invited the Clan of Others to participate in harvesting the fish from the fish trap.

Taelo's father, Grey Fox Running, had invited the clan of Others to attend the late season meeting of all the Elk sub-clans.

The teeth from a giant shark they caught in their fish trap and the salt they made from the sea water made all of them very well to do young men.

Then White Swan and Quiet Pheasant had arranged for the current long hunt he and the team were on. It was her attempt to change the culture of her clan and raise the status of women in her clan.

It was hard to keep up with the events that surrounded Taelo.

He felt Meadow Flower's hand as she ran it down his shoulder. Her action brought him out of his reminiscing. He watched Taelo and Quiet Rabbit slowly cull out the mother buffalo and the very late young calf. He knew Taelo had some ulterior motive for rescuing the young calf, but it escaped him what it might be.

Meadow Flower asked him why Taelo had not spoken up about killing four buffalo when Little Otter was boasting about Golden Hawk's success at killing four buffalo.

In fact, Taelo had not only killed four buffalo but had dropped each of them so close to the forest that their team's processing was almost done when Golden Hawk's first buffalo was hoisted into the trees.

He replied to her question by making the point that Taelo was completely confident in himself and did not seek the compliments of others.

He pointed out that Golden Hawk had the same attitude.

He made the observation that the two were complements of each other.

He jumped up as he watched Taelo take the young calf down and tie its feet. He was momentarily afraid the mother buffalo was going to attack but then he watched Quiet Rabbit bravely jump up with her spear in one hand and a piece of leather in the other. Her action stopped the mother buffalo, and it retreated as Quiet Rabbit continued her advance.

He commented to Meadow Flower that the mother buffalo could have easily run over Quiet Rabbit had it been more aggressive.

Meadow Flower responded that Quiet Rabbit would have knelt and placed the spear to the buffalo's chest.

She had half expected her to have killed the ninth buffalo. She pointed out that not only was Quiet Rabbit, brave she was fast, and she had learned a new and deadly skill.

After Taelo returned with the young buffalo and tied it to one of the trees. He went over to where Golden Hawk's team was still processing their kill.

Burley Bear went with Taelo and together they pulled in the other three buffalo that Golden Hawk had killed.

Golden Hawk almost immediately noted and complemented Taelo on his success and thanked him for his help.

This exchange had stopped Little Otter in mid-sentence as he realized that Taelo had also killed four buffalo and the work of processing those four was done.

Meadow Flower commented that eight buffalo far exceeded her expectation of how successful they would be. She said that it was hard for her to believe that anyone could run as fast as either Taelo or Golden Hawk. She had been amazed that Quiet Rabbit and Busy Bee had both kept up and had been able to carry the extra spears.

She commented on the fact that she was stronger than any of the new ones, but she certainly would never be able to move as fast as they did.

Burley Bear jokingly commented that she only had to run fast enough to catch him, and he would make sure he always ran slow enough to get caught.

Meadow Flower thought back to only a few sun's ago, when she had been surprised when Broken Spear, the Clan's seer approached her and told her that she should prepare to go on a long hunt with a long hunt group made up of the New Ones and Burley Bear. He explained that the group was a mix of young men and women. These young men and women did not know it, but this long hunt would bond them for life.

Each would find a mate.

He saw her as the mate for Burley Bear.

Meadow Flower laughed and told Broken Spear that a seer was not needed to make the connection between her and Burley Bear. The two of them were life-long friends and had promised to be one another's mate when they were only eight seasons old. \\

Every year the two of them would walk through the forest holding hands. They would comment on having passed another cycle of seasons and discuss what they had learned. They would again verify that they still were on track to spend all the coming seasons together.

She stopped and thanked Broken Spear for having crystalized the situation and for making the bond official. This would make it easy for her father Quiet Fox to accept Burley Bear. He had always questioned her devotion and belief in him.

Quiet Rabbit's groan as she followed Taelo and the young calf into the forest brought Meadow Flower back to the present.

She took the two spears Quiet Rabbit was carrying and took her over to the fire where she had a piece of the buffalo hump roasting.

It was clear to her that Quiet Rabbit had used the last bit of her energy to go out with Taelo.

During the race to determine who would be put on each team, she had watched Quiet Rabbit accelerate and pass Busy Bee and Talking Wren as if they were standing still. It was clear to her who Taelo's mate was to be.

She realized that race had been at the beginning of this sun cycle and Quiet Rabbit had been going full steam for the entire time.

She put stamina on the list of things the two different clans had in common.

Burley Bear followed Taelo. He went out with Taelo and helped him bring two long branches to make into a heavy-duty travois. The two branches would easily carry a buffalo.

He let out a little laugh of disbelief when Taelo told him the travois was for the young buffalo he had captured.

He soon swallowed that same a laugh when Taelo began to make a harness like the one Burley Bear had made for the three of them to pull the sled with three buffalo on it.

He realized and was amazed that Taelo had extrapolated the idea of harnessing a human to a sled to doing so with a buffalo.

The young buffalo fought the arrangement but by the time the sun was ready to descent behind the far mountains Taelo, and Little Otter had pulled four buffalo and hung them just outside of their main campsite.

While the meat was being pulled in, Burley Bear and Golden Hawk arranged a pen that would hold the young buffalo. They agreed that the young buffalo deserved to be guarded.

They were relieved when Little Otter and Talking Wren volunteered to stay up and guard it.

Burley Bear was not sure he could have stayed awake to properly guard anything. He barely had the energy to climb up into his sleeping area in the tree.

The young buffalo proved to be invaluable. Burley Bear, Meadow Flower, Quiet Rabbit and Busy Bee processed and packaged most of the meat while Taelo, Golden Hawk and Little

Otter brought the meat in. The last load included a young boar that Golden Hawk had surprised and killed.

Marigold excused herself from the processing of the last buffalo and proceeded to prepare the young boar for a celebration dinner.

During the celebration dinner the team decided that they should send the first load of meat back to both the Cave of the Others and the Elk Camp.

Little Otter volunteered to take the meat back. He claimed the young bull was attached to him.

Burley Bear had a good laugh when he learned that Little Otter had named the young bull Little Burley after himself and Burley Bear. Little Otter claimed the young bull had demonstrated the strength of both of them.

When Talking Wren volunteered to accompany Little Otter, Marigold commented that would mean the hunters would have some peace and quiet.

She kept quiet as Quiet Rabbit commented that Talking Wren's company would follow Taelo's rule of always having a partner during the hunt. It was clear to her that the whole team agreed and looked forward to a few days of quiet.

The two hunt teams continued to hunt. Marigold went with Golden Hawk and Burley Bear continued to support Taelo.

Burley Bear commented that Taelo and Golden Hawk had changed their focus to hunting a more diverse mix of animals.

They were bringing in many deer, elk, wild boar, and a host of smaller game.

Meadow Flower agreed but pointed out that the quantity still exceeded what she had expected. It appeared to her that by the time Little Otter returned it would be time to send a second load of meat back to both clans.

A few sun cycles later a long hunter from her clan came into camp with the news that a crazed saber tooth tiger had attacked his team.

He announced that Rolling Stone had been slashed across the chest and might not make it.

Meadow Flower reacted with emotion. Rolling Stone was a friend. He was to her sister what Burley Bear was to her.

Rolling Stone was a friend of Burley Bear and he would have left immediately had Taelo not intervened.

It was dark. There was no moon. If a saber tooth tiger was out then they would be easy targets.

Taelo suggested letting the long hunt messenger get a good night sleep and, in the morning, the entire team would go to rescue the other long hunters.

That night Burley Bear awoke to the putrid smell of death. It was very early in the morning, and the sun was threatening to rise over the far distant mountains.

Suddenly an ear-splitting roar came from where Taelo had his sleeping area.

With spear in hand, Burley Bear jumped down from his sleeping area. He watched as Taelo recovered from his fall out of the tree. Taelo's spear was lying next to a monstrous saber tooth tiger that was also recovering from the fall.

Burley Bear began shouting and whooping in an attempt to distract the tiger.

He watched as Taelo also began yelling and then turned and ran out of camp. The saber tooth seemed to reject him and went after Taelo.

Burley Bear followed the two. He was yelling as loudly as possible in hopes of distracting the saber tooth.

He watched as the saber tooth slowly closed the gap to Taelo. He was not sure if Taelo would make it to the lake.

Burley Bear was shocked when Quiet Rabbit passed him as she yelled at the top of her voice. He watched as she slowly closed the gap to the tiger and Taelo.

He wondered what she would do when she caught up. He could not keep pace. It was clear to him that Quiet Rabbit was very likely to catch up with Taelo and the tiger.

He arrived and found a bewildered Quiet Rabbit that was frantically calling for Taelo.

For a short period, they could not locate Taelo.

Burley Bear thanked the ancients for Taelo's miraculous survival. He and the tiger fell down into a water filled chimney hole.

Taelo had found an alternate way out, but the dead tiger was floating down in the water.

Quiet Rabbit volunteered to be lowered into the dark chimney and tie a rope to the tiger. This cemented Burley Bear's opinion that she had to be one of the bravest persons he had ever met.

The rise of the sun gave light to the morning as he, Meadow Flower and the lead hunter of the Others lifted the tiger from the shaft.

He then dropped the rope back down into the dark shaft and single handedly pulled Quiet Rabbit out of the shaft.

Once the tiger was hanging in the tree, Burley bear led the team to rescue his friend.

He was shocked at the condition that he found Rolling Stone. The five deep slashes of the tiger across his chest exposed the chest bones.

His first reaction was to wish his friend a smooth way to the ancients.

He pulled Marigold out of the way and stepped back as Quiet Rabbit knelt next to Rolling Stone.

She carefully examined each slash. Then she washed out the wound with salt and water mixture.

She then coated each slash with honey.

She carefully arranged the flaps of skin and flesh.

Then she stitched the deep part of each slash wound. She began with the gut thread knots on the outside and ended the inner stitching with the end also knotted to the outside.

Finally, he watched her stitch the top of the gash, so the edges were just touching each other. He made the observation that the scars would heal with a smooth exterior.

Meadow Flower watched Quiet Rabbit and asked about each step. She asked where Quiet Rabbit had learned how to treat such cuts.

Quiet Rabbit thought for a moment and said that she had learned to clean wounds from her mother and good sewing techniques from her grandmother. She had put them together for the first time when she saw the wounds on Rolling Stones chest.

She had figured out how to make sure the thread for the deep stitches could be pulled out by watching Taelo and Golden Hawk handle their ropes during their cliff climbing during the spring egg gathering.

Meadow Flower looked up at Burley Bear, raised one eyebrow and quietly commented that maybe she should not have asked.

Rolling Stone opened his eyes. He asked where he was. When asked how he felt, he commented that he felt better.

Quiet Rabbit put her hand to his chest and told him he was safe; the tiger was dead, and he would get the best care. She told him that sleep was the best medicine.

Rolling Stone seemed to relax and fall asleep.

Burley Bear had the entire long hunt team of the Others return to the cave. He assured them that the clan would have all the meat they would need, and they should recover and then make sure Rolling Stone got what he needed.

He knew that the Valley of Plenty had a wealth of buffalo, and this long hunt was one that White Swan and Silent Pheasant had used to enhance the standing of women in the Elk Clan.

Two sun cycles later, Meadow Flower looked up the valley to the water cascading down the cliff and the steam rising from the warm water pool. She was leading the hunt team back. She planned to explain the care that her sister Marigold was to give to Rolling Stone and then she would return to the hunt.

Quiet Rabbit had insisted she accompany Rolling Stone back to the cave.

Taelo had agreed and highlighted the safety factor and that there should always be two traveling together.

Meadow Flower had agreed. Her main concern was to get Rolling Stone back to the safety and the care he would get at the cave.

Marigold was startled by the pale look on Rolling Stone's face.

Broken Spear looked at the wound and complimented Quiet Rabbit when he found out she had sealed the gashes. He commented on the excellent repair work she had done on Rolling Stone and said that had she been around when the bear mauled him, he might have been much better looking.

He went on to state that Rolling Stone, like himself, had earned a new name. He would be called Saber Scar for the marks on his chest.

Meadow Flower and Quiet Rabbit enjoyed the hot pool and a solid relaxed, night's rest. At sunrise they packed their gear and started their journey back to the area they expected to find the long hunt team.

They arrived to find the camp had been cleared and a stone signal pointed the way to where the team was heading.

Quiet Rabbit became anxious when she saw the drawing of a mastodon in the dirt by the stone marker.

She stepped up the pace to catch up to Taelo.

Burley Bear was surprised by Taelo's decision to move. He had come back with the news of a very large mastodon herd that he wanted to follow.

When the team decided to kill one mastodon, he knew that the hunt team would set a record for the amount of meat a long hunt team would bring back.

Taelo and Golden Hawk pointed to the fact that bringing back the meat of a mastodon would be a first for the Elk Clan. They also pointed out that their long hunt team would be breaking all records for the amount of meat brought in.

Their plan was to follow the herd but only bag deer, elk, boar, and any other small animal they came across.

They would hunt the mastodon when Meadow Flower and Quiet Rabbit returned. This would allow the entire team to participate in what might be a once in a lifetime experience.

Two sun cycles passed before Burley Bear spotted two joggers approaching. The pair made up of a large jogger and one that was smaller than her shadow at the sun's zenith could only be Quiet Rabbit and his Meadow Flower.

He called for a stop and began putting together a cooking ring. He put pieces of boar meat on a spit, salted it and put it over the hot coals.

He had praised Taelo for the decision to wait on hunting the mastodon. Now as he watched the two joggers, he felt the team would be successful.

Quiet Rabbit commented to Meadow Flower that the hunt team had stopped early. Meadow Flower replied that she was sure Burley Bear had spotted them and made the call to stop.

Quiet Rabbit was surprised by the salted boar and roasted onion dinner. She complemented Burley Bear for being so quick and so good at having something to eat.

His smile, which always reminded her of a grimace, was indication that he liked the compliment.

The next sunrise Taelo, Golden Hawk and Quiet Rabbit set out to select a young bull mastodon. It did not surprise him when Quiet Rabbit returned to lead the team to where Taelo and Golden Hawk were to guide a single mastodon.

She was anxious that the team leave as early at the next sunrise as possible. She was worried that Taelo and Golden Hawk might not be able to wait on the whole team.

Burley Bear reassured her that Taelo would wait for the whole team to participate.

He and Meadow flower were again impressed at Taelo's and Golden Hawks ingenuity when they saw the trap that the two had devised to capture a mastodon.

He and his clan had hunted mastodon before. Their hunt style required a cliff that they could run the mastodon over. Another more dangerous technique was to surround the animal and wear it out by repeatedly making it rear up by attacking it.

He lauded Taelo and Golden Hawk for having successfully trapped the mastodon into a tight, steep sided ravine.

He felt especially honored when he was asked to be the one to spear the animal through the heart.

He almost dropped his spear when on the other side of the ravine, Little Otter slipped and started to slide down into the ravine.

He watched as Talking Wren grabbed Little Otter's hair and pulled him back up the slope.

He plunged his spear just behind and above the front leg of the mastodon. Meadow Flower who had taken Little Otter's spear did the same from the other side.

He and the rest of the team let out a shout as the mastodon went down on its knees. It had died almost immediately.

Burley Bear decided that each hunting technique had it good and its bad. Getting the mastodon back out of the ravine took much more effort than any of the team had anticipated.

Their share of the long hunt would be more than any team hunters of Others had ever harvested. He and Meadow Flower would be among the most prolific long hunters in their clan's verbal history.

The travois pulled by the young buffalo made it possible to pull all the meat and choice pieces of the mastodon. Their additional meat and numerous hides were pulled on three travois by two team members on each travois.

Burley Bear and Meadow Flower were always on separate travois. He thanked Taelo for having arranged it so the two of them could walk together during their break from pulling.

He shared with her the fact that he had celebrated throughout the night when he had found out that she was to accompany him as his hunting partner. The fact that Broken Spear had announced this long hunt made up of paired mates had saved him from having to ask Quiet Fox for her hand.

Meadow Flower asked if as big as he was, was he afraid of her father.

He replied that he was not afraid of him but of his possible rejection. Such a position would have forced his hand.

Meadow Flower stopped and gave Burley Bear a hug.

Taelo stopped at the same time and commented that he thought only Burley Bear's mother loved him enough to hug him.

Burley Bear laughed and agreed that for a long time he had thought the same thing.

He then pointed to Meadow Flower and said she had given him her friendship and the confidence to weather all challenges.

Soon after the long hunt was over, Burley Bear went with the Elk Clan as the Clan of Others joined together to attend the gathering in the valley where the eagle and Broken Spear had first watched the very young Taelo, standing on the naming hide, holding up the eagle's claw.

He was aware that the two clans had arrived early in order to set up camp on the far side of the lake. The presence of the Others at the Elk Clan gathering was certain to raise many questions and certainly some objections.

At the first meeting of the Elk Clan council, he listened to the eloquent description Grey Fox Running gave of the Clan of Others. He went on to describe the role of women in the Clan of Others and that the Elk Clan had elected White Swan, Quiet Pheasant and Floating Cloud to the Elk Clan leadership council. This raised numerous objections.

Grey Fox Running, named Golden Hawk, Taelo and himself as hunters of the clan. Taelo's and Golden Hawk's age gave rise to a host of objections.

Quite Fox announced that his clan had also made both of them hunters in the Clan of Others.

Wise Owl, the overall leader for the meeting had to ask for silence. He made that point that the Elk Clan had left the last meeting in a desperate situation. In one season they had returned with wealth that exceeded that of all the other clans put together.

He pointed to the salt, the fish, the buffalo meat and hides that were freely being distributed to each clan. He asked that all the Elk sub-clan leaders should think about what this meant and what message the Ancients were trying to send to them.

He, Taelo and Golden Hawk were in the dark outside of the meeting area. They commented on the power that Wise Owl had just demonstrated. They knew they had made a significant contribution to the direction of all the Elk Clans.

On the return to the Elk Camp by the seashore, Taelo described a trip to the south, a trip that he offered to all the members of the hunt team.

There was an immediate acceptance. The team wanted to have another experience together.

The Long hunt had bonded them.

A new adventure, Burley Bear was sure, would give them a new reason for tightening that bond.

He would follow Taelo anywhere.

He and Meadow Flower were where they wanted to be.

The End

Saber Scar & Merigold

S aber Scar had returned to visit the place where his name had changed from Rolling Stone and he unwillingly had become Saber Scar.

The attack of a crazed saber tooth tiger had almost ended his life.   He survived because of sewing skill, and the care he got from his soul mate.

Marigold, his soul mate, sat next to him.

His most cherished friends with whom he had adventured around the world sat around the celebration fire ring.

The closest to him was Quite Rabbit who twice had put him back together.   Her skill at treating him was why he was sitting and enjoying the day.

The first time she had put him back together was at the exact spot where they all sat.   She had sewn closed the five saber tigers claw mark across his chest.   He ran his hand over the five smooth scars and recalled his later amazement to be alive.

He remembered that concerned look on Marigold's face when back at the Cave and he finally opened his eyes.

He was amazed that he had survived.

After his recovery, he had traveled with Taelo and the rest of the team to the land of the condor.

Then he had travelled north and crossed the ice bridge and fought the Sky Eyes.

On the return he and Burley Bear had played a big part in rescuing Taelo and his wolf team.   It was one of the few times that Taelo needed saving.

On that same trip, he had watched in amazement as Taelo rescued Single Leaf from drowning.

He knew that Single Leaf and Taelo had a ceremonial dinner, when the clans gathered, with the old Weaver who had taught Taelo how to rescue a drowning person.   That was the repayment price Taelo put on saving Single Leaf.   He smiled at what Taelo specified as the cost of saving her and he had teased Single Leaf about the fact that she had gotten off very easily.   Had he saved her she would be cooking a cleaning his hearth for the rest of her life.

He found Taelo looking at him, smiling.

Taelo was the person who inspired him.   Taelo had saved his life multiple times and he had shown him how a powerful, self-confident person behaved.

It was a behavior that he had adopted.

He accepted the fact that he would never be a Taelo but he would be the self-confident person that Taelo had grown him to become.

He had now traveled around the world and on the beginning to that trip he had suffered another slash across his chest.

This time it was a giant lion. He had been saved by Feather-in-the-Wind who had used her body as a spear to knock the lion aside.

But the Lion managed to add a fresh set of claw marks across his chest.

Once again he was sure that he had received a fatal blow.

He had opened his eyes to look into Quite Rabbit's eyes and he knew at that instant that he was going to survive.

However, he drank heavily of the white lightening that Taelo had him drink and it was hours until he once again opened his eyes and looked into Marigold's worried eyes.

Then after he was able to travel, they had crossed the mighty river where he had fallen off the raft and was about to drown.

He became the second Other to be saved from drowning by Taelo.

He had since attended every ceremonial dinner with the Weaver. It was a very enjoyable dinner that he and Single Leaf prepared together.

Single leaf had teased him about how easily he had gotten off and that she would have had him hunt for her every day until he was old and feeble.

Taelo had laughed and added that both of them would too soon be old and feeble and they should focus on the here and now. They should focus on helping those that needed their help and on making sure that those they helped, helped others.

He next looked at Feather-in-the-Wind and Running Stag. Both of them had been with him when they were attacked by the giant lion. Together they had saved him. They now led the Paradise Elk Clan. They both owed their lives to Taelo and Quiet Rabbit.

Feather-in-the-Wind had been saved by Quiet Rabbit and Busy Bee from being a frozen princess offering to the Condor.

Then she had been protected by Taelo, from the Warrior Clan leader who wanted her as his bride.

Feather-in-the-Wind had been in the battle with the Sky Eyes and had led the wolf attack. She later befriended the Bear Clan members and when she was selected to lead a new clan she took in all the young men and women who had not been selected by the other clans.

She had a loyal following that revered her.

He took note that she was wearing the outfit that Marigold had made for her from the giant lion skin. He noted that Running Stag was also wearing his outfit.

He smiled as he realized the three of them were in their lion outfits.

Feather-in-the-Wind looked fragile but was fearless and ferocious in battle. He smiled as he thought about the transition from Condor Princess to the Queen of the Paradise Elk Clan.

He looked at Running Stag and knew that he was as fearless, and as brave and that he was a perfect match for Feather-in-the-Wind.

Running Stag had fought with Taelo to rescue his parents from the cannibals.

In a later battle against a superior number of Cannibals he had fought and been wounded but had kept them from attacking from the cliff side.

It was Quiet Rabbit that had sewn the slash on Running Stags back and it was done while he was wide awake. He had not even groaned. He was tough.

In the rescue, that they now called the Lasher rescue, Running Stag had led three loaded sleds of people being rescued through a blinding snow storm and saved everyone. Running Stag credited Lasher as the hero of that ride.

Running Stag had accomplished this before he was considered an adult.

Taelo made sure that he was recognized as the youngest warrior in Elk Clan history.

Saber Scar took looked up at the sun at its zenith. He felt the brisk breeze as it swept across the valley and bent the tall yellow drying grass. The smell of the roasting boar that was making his mouth water brought him out of his renaissance to once again focus on the gathering..

He watched as Marigold spread honey across the back and sides of the boar as she got ready to remove it from the fire.

He stood up and took one end of the spit and saw that Taelo was on the other side picking up the other end. Together they placed it on the waiting holder.

He extracted the muscle along the back bone and cut off a large piece and presented it to Taelo.

He then went around and gave everyone a section of the choice pieces from the boar. He made a point of thanking each person for having been a treasure in his life and coming to this humble event where he had first earned the name Saber Scar.

Marigold had been observing her mate as he sat quietly as his guests talked with each other around the cooking fire. She knew that this was her mate's way, as Feather-in-the-Wind was known to say, "get back on the Llama that has thrown you off."

Saber Scar had over the years struggled with the fact that he had not been the one that had kill the Saber Tooth tigress that had marked him.

She had seen Taelo and Quiet Rabbit put the pair of Saber teeth in a rabbit pouch. She was not surprised when the two, Golden Hawk and Busy Bee stood and presented the pouch to him.

She was, however, astonished when he opened the bag and took the first tooth out.   It had an intricate carving of a black saber tooth on each side.

When he took out the second tooth the carving on each side was that of a tan colored lion.

It was clear to her that, Taelo, Quiet Rabbit, Golden Hawk and Busy Bee had spent a great deal of time preparing such a gift.

Feather-in-the-Wind stood and presented him with her knife that he had used to repeatedly stab the lion.

Running Stag presented him with the bow and the arrows that he had used to shoot the lion.   He wished him better luck if he had to shoot a lion with arrows.

There was a hush around the circle.

Then Burley Bear let out the war cry that he and Taelo used. The entire group followed his lead and let out a war cry.   Then he lifted two large bags of honey wine and suggested they all eat and drink as much as they could.

Meadow Flower suggested they eat and drink everything so there would be nothing to take back to the Cave of Others.

The setting sun painted the horizon a crimson purple, red and yellow as it reached the horizon and was ready to set.

High overhead an eagle let out its call.   They all knew that Broken Spear had been watching the celebration.

It was a fitting end to Saber Scar's celebration and resurgence.

The End

Taelo Character Stories

179

Taelo Character Stories

<u>Broken Spear</u>

*L*ong Spear walked the narrow trail and took in the light blue sky that outlined the edge of the craggily jagged cliff with evergreen trees clinging to its face rising high above him.   He was following a small river looking for a likely place to spear fish or with even better luck catch a nice sized turtle.

This was a day to relax and enjoy.

It was the last of the warm weather before the cold once again took hold.

His return on the previous sun cycle from a very successful hunt left him at ease about the amount of food the clan had available.   He and his hunting team would remain in camp for at least one moon cycle before the next hunt.   This would give him and his hunters ample time to recover.

His mate had enthusiastically welcomed him back with both a specially prepared meal and the surprise announcement that he would soon have another mouth to feed.   This had made him feel grand.

He looked forward to raising the child and passing on the stories that his parents had told him.

He felt on top of the world.

Ahead of him the path dipped where a small side stream came in at the opposite side of the river. The rapids above this point ran down into a still placid pool of water. Long Spear crossed at the top of the rapids by springing from stone to stone. He was pleased to make it across with dry feet. Once across he cautiously approached the pool.

His stealth had paid off.

A large fish was lazily holding its position in the pool. It looked to be asleep but Long Spear figured the large fish was probably waiting for small unsuspecting fish to come down the rapids directly into its mouth.

He slowly raised his spear, aimed his throw to just below the fish and then let the spear fly. He immediately jumped in, pushed the spear all the way through and lifted the arm sized fish out of the water.

So much for his dry feet, he thought as a grin spread across his face.

After gutting the fish, he found and cut off a small stout willow about the thickness of his thumb and ran it length wise through the fish.

He was now ready to carry his prize home and enjoy a mid-sun cycle meal.

He remained on the side of the river opposite from the path he had followed along the base of the cliff. From his new vantage, he was able to see the entrance to the cave that went far back into the cliff. This cave was known as the Children's Cave.

An extremely narrow passage prevented any of the much larger adults to go back to a very large cavern just beyond that point. In his younger years he had made the journey to that back room. It had been many cycles of seasons since he had last been able to squeeze beyond that narrow entrance.

The calm wide and shallow pool at the base of the cliff just below the cave entrance was a favorite spot for families with small children to spend a sunny summer day. The parents would relax on the sandy flat bank while the children frolicked in the pool.

Just a short distance up the river from the Children's Cave was a large open cave that served as the meeting place for the clan leadership. This was known as the Leader's Cave and was generally off limits to everyone but those in the leadership position.

This was where he and his hunt team would come and organize each hunt. The hunt teams were given their instructions and the clan Seer would share any message he might have received from the Ancients.

Long Spear was a sceptic as it regarded the Ancients. He did not believe the Seer spoke to anyone other than those present before him. He could not remember one message or piece of advice a Seer had ever given to him or anyone else that had been of any relevance. He kept his skepticism to himself, but he was sure the "Seer" was that in name only.

He instead always made sure those going on the hunt with him were well prepared. Then as they went to the hunting grounds, he would lead them in discussions on how to handle any emergency that might arise.

He would then discuss the hunting strategy for that specific hunt.

All this went through his head as he turned up the path away from the cliff and the river toward the area where the clan was camped.

The Bear Clan's camp was neatly organized. He and his friend Silver Arrow had arranged the camp layout. He had insisted that the members of the clan keep the area clean and free of waste. This had won him the praise of the leadership council.

Long Spear enjoyed watching his mate, Tall Fern. She had seen the fish he was carrying and had immediately put wood into the cooking ring. The hot coals from the morning fire quickly re-established a perfect flame to do the grilling.

The pole the fish was on was long enough to reach across the two supports on each side of the fire. Tall Fern peeled the willow bark from the thick end and tied it in such a fashion that it made a handle so she could turn the fish over the fire.

She complemented Long Spear on bringing home such a nice mid sun cycle treat. She rubbed salt on the fish as she slowly rotated it. She knew it would not take long before they would enjoy their meal.

Long Spear relaxed and watched. He knew that Tall Fern was a good match for him. He had always been very shy and had found it hard to be around most of the young women. She on the other hand, though very good looking had always been too aggressive and had scared away most of her potential mates.

Somehow, she had noticed him and had decided that he would be a perfect mate for her. He had been very happy to have been her target.

Long Spear had been pleased with being her choice. He was one of the few people that consistently stood up to her. When he agreed the world was peaceful. When he did not agree and stood his ground, the world around him often rumbled.

He thought of their partnership as one that would keep the seasons ahead of them interesting and alive.

A few sun cycles later he and his best friend and normal hunt partner, Silver Arrow, were asked to take out a group of the younger, eager members of the clan for their first hunt.

This was an honor and recognition for them. They readily agreed.

He and Silver Arrow discussed where they should take their young hunter trainees. They decided on a valley that they felt would have many elk and if they were lucky there would also be some buffalo.

The group consisted of twelve young hunters. This made it one of the larger hunt teams. Long Spear would have preferred half the number. It would take a little more effort on his and Silver Arrow's part, but they would teach each of the group their hunter survival skills and how to hunt together successfully.

He led the way at a fast pace and discussed the hunting approach he planned to use.

Silver Arrow augmented his teaching and explained how each hunter was expected to take part.

Long Spear would create a large hunt circle and have it slowly close-in toward its center.

Any animals trying to escape would be targeted and be speared.

On the third sun cycle, he came to a crest overlooking a valley and could see an abundance of elk mixed with buffalo grazing on the tall grasses.

Long Spear assigned the members to their locations and then sent them out to create a large circle. He instructed them on how to handle the elk and the buffalo. Each animal would act differently but each would be trying to break out of the circle.

The action each hunter had to carry out was to spear the animal and then follow through with a strike to the side of the head with their stone headed clubs.

Once everyone was in position, Long Spear gave the signal to start closing the circle. The circle was slowly tightened until the animals realized they were surrounded. The buffalo herd seemed to sense the situation and moved in unison as they followed the lead buffalo.

Long Spear and two of his young hunters were able to bring down a young buffalo that was on the way past them.

Silver Arrow had similar success on his side of the herd.

Two other hunters successfully downed a large female elk. They were shouting and dancing around their kill.

Long Spear complimented the two hunters on their kill but pointed out that all twelve of them had contributed equally. It had been their cooperation that had led them to a successful first hunt encounter.

Two buffalo and one large elk was almost enough for the hunt team to return to their home camp.

Long Spear and Silver Arrow showed the team how to field dress the three animals. They were gutted and the desirable inner organs were put in the animal's chest cavity. They then had the animals pulled to the edge of the forest and hoisted into the trees.

Long Spear decide that the team would follow the herd and see if they could once again experience success. He asked the two hunters that had downed the elk to stay and keep predators away from the animals that had been killed. He rewarded them by leaving them each some salt and a tender tongue to roast.

The team caught up with the herd and was able to take down an additional buffalo.

Long Spear decided that three buffalo and an elk was enough for the team to pull back to their valley.

Four travois were needed for the return trip.

Now Long Spear felt good about having the large number young hunters with him.

He assigned two persons to each travois. The extra four persons would rotate into a pulling position every one-hundred spear throw lengths.

This would make sure each person got several periods of rest as they made their return.   This would allow him to maintain a fast pace back to the village.

Along the way, the way as the sun reached its zenith the team spotted a black berry patch that was loaded with berries.

Long Spear called for a halt. He pointed to the black berry patch and said the team could indulge while he roasted some meat for their meal.

There was a rush into the berry patch by the eager hunters.

He had just put the meat over the fire when a roar that seemed to shake the ground caused Long Spear to grab his weapons and run toward the berry patch.

Standing at least two spears high was the largest bear Long Spear had ever encountered. He noted that she had a notch missing from one ear. Her teeth seemed to be as long as his fingers. A cub the size of a normal bear was eating berries and seemed to be watching its mother.

He knew he had to distract her before she attacked the unarmed hunters. Only one of them had a spear.

Long Spear was standing behind the giant bear. She had her back to him and was getting ready to charge the group of young hunters that seemed frozen in place. Long Spear quietly told them to begin to slowly back away from the bear.

He had no sooner given the instruction when the bear turned and charged him.

The world and his movements seemed to go into slow motion. The giant mother bear pawed his spear aside as easily as he swatted flies and continued her charge. He now was only armed with his skinning blade and knew that he was in mortal in close combat.

The bear ran over him. He fell flat on his back and immediately tried to turn over.

But a giant paw on his back pushed him flat.

He rolled and managed to stand and face her as she stood upright.

He put each of his feet on one of her back paws and leaned backwards. He was trying to pull her down.

The two of them fell slowly.

He tried to twist as he fell to get out from under her, but her size and weight prevented him from doing so.

He heard the cracking of his leg bones as they hit the ground and she stepped on his calves.

The bear now took his entire head in her mouth. He could hear the cracking of his skull as she shook his head.

He continued to repeatedly stab her with his skinning blade.

He knew he had reached the end of his journey as the world went dark.

He had lost the battle.

He instinctively kept trying to stab the bear.

Silver Arrow had only been one step behind Long Spear. He immediately attacked the giant bear.

She let go of what now appeared to be a dead opponent and stood back up and let out another roar.

Silver Arrow slowly backed away from the berry patch. He watched as the mother bear shook her head and came down on all four.

She sniffed Long Spear's body.

It was clear by the blood dripping from her fur that she had received multiple stab wounds from Long Spear. She sniffed her cub, turned towards the opposite side from Silver Arrow and left the berry patch.

Silver Arrow rushed forward to inspect Long Spear. He was surprised to find him still breathing. Long Spear's legs were badly broken. His face was mutilated, and his scalp was torn open.

Silver Arrow splinted the broken leg bones as best he could, but the bones were shattered. He closed the scalp wound but the scars on Long Spear's face needed more than Silver Arrow could do in the field.

Silver Arrow put one of the hunters in charge of bringing the meat from the hunt back to the camp.

He and the person he believed had the most stamina would pull a travois with Long Spear on it and return to the main camp as quickly as they could.

Once he had made the arrangements and had Long Spear on the travois, he set out at the fastest pace he could maintain. He planned to keep moving throughout the night and until he reached the Bear Clan camp.

The sun was just rising as he hailed the camp. He pulled the travois directly to Long Spear's lodge.

He watched as Tall Fern took one look and went into her hutch and returned with her sewing materials. She asked for someone to get some clean fresh water.

Silver Arrow was surprised. He had not expected such a controlled reaction.

In what seemed a bright warm world, Long Spear realized he was talking to several family members who he knew had gone to the next world. He wondered whether he was in this new world with them.

They let him know that it was not yet his time.

He was totally disoriented. He could not remember what he had been doing. He wondered about the meaning of his conversation with those he knew were in the next world.

He opened his eyes and was looking directly at the worried eyes of Tall Fern. She was trying to put some liquid food in his mouth. He took the salty, thick fluid in and swallowed. It was warm and tasted very good.

He asked where he was. Then he remembered the bear and asked if anyone else had been hurt.

He was relieved that no one else had been hurt. He asked about the bear and learned that it had survived.

Silver Arrow was sitting by the fire as he watched his friend come back to life. His friend was a much-changed person. The thought of a Broken Spear came to mind.

He welcomed Long Spear back to the land of the living. He let him know that it had been almost ten sun cycles since he had fought the bear. He explained that the bear had left the berry patch in a wounded condition but that it seemed she would survive.

Silver Arrow made the point that Long Spear had saved the rest of the hunt team.

Long Spear felt the scar from the back right-side of his head to the point where it ended on his left chin. He then ran his fingers along each of the other gashes that seemed to randomly cross his face.

He wanted to go to the stream to get a view of his mutilated head and face.

The pain from his legs let him know that he would not soon be getting up to walk.

He evaluated the splints on his leg. The swelling was going down. He realized that the bones had not just been broken but some seemed to have been crushed. He wondered if he would ever walk again.

Tall Fern kept the news of her loss of their child to herself. She knew her mate faced a major challenge in recovering from his wounds and did not need any additional stress. He would soon come to realize the loss.

She noted that the winter seemed to be very dismal, cold, and dark. It was very much how she felt. She thought back to just a few sun cycles ago when they had enjoyed the fish he had brought back from the stream.

It now seemed to be a lifetime ago.

Long Spear rapidly recovered from his head wounds, but his legs would never function as they had before. He knew that he would require a crutch to move about. He also knew he would never hunt again.

He began to evaluate what he could do that would be of value to the clan.

By the time the warmth of spring became noticeable, he had become aware that he would not be a father. This disappointed him but he took it in stride.

He was now more worried about Tall Fern. She seemed to have suffered a great deal by the loss of her pregnancy. She had lost her fighting spirit.

At about this same time, Long Spear began to realize that he could see through the eyes of various animals. The hawk, the crow and the eagle all seemed to accommodate his presence.

Long Spear spent several moon cycles experimenting with this new-found capability. He followed hunt teams as they went on their springtime hunts. He followed the animal herds and participated in the eagle's hunt for its food.

He kept all of this to himself. He did not want to scare Tall Fern or the other clan members.

It was an exhilarating feeling and one that gave him knowledge and a vision of the surrounding territory that he had never had before.

He began using his new capability to help the hunt teams find their prey.

He was soon being sought out by the hunt leaders for his advice.

His new skill was noted. The leadership team asked him to participate in the leadership council.

He was personally pleased with this new capability that allowed him to add value to the well-being of the clan.

Then a second shock hit him.

Tall Fern became ill and in less than a handful of sun cycles she was gone. He had fed her, kept her warm but nothing seemed to help.

He sent her on to the next world and wondered why it had to be so.

Her departure marked the beginning of his conversations with the Ancients. His previous doubts evaporated. He knew that he either had lost his mind or he was truly communicating with those who were in the next world.

He chose to test out this new capability. He began to test the ability of the Ancients to give him useful insights.

He was able to give a hunt party warning about a pack of dire wolves and how to defend against them.

When events unfolded as he had described, he was elevated to the position of Seer.

It was during this ceremony that he was renamed Broken Spear and had the title of Bear Clan Seer attached to it. He did not immediately take to this new name but the more he thought about it the more appropriate it became.

He continued to develop his capabilities and was focused on only sharing what he knew he had seen or what he believed was true. He did not want to misrepresent what he knew. He would often respond to a request with the simple statement that he did not know.

He was aware of his growing influence and status.

This did not help him with courting the women and he did not take a new mate.

Instead, he took in several older women that had lost their mates. They were grateful to him and gave him the care that he needed.

This arrangement allowed him to concentrate on his new responsibility as the Bear Clan Seer.

Many seasons passed and his status grew. There were no other Seers in the clan. The clan had been doing well but for some reason the number of new children kept declining.

He consulted the Ancients in an attempt to understand what was happening.

The Ancients instructed him to fly with the eagle. He was told that he would see a leader that would lead the clan to a new future.

He was in the mind of the eagle as it crested the edge of the valley. He took in the oblong lake below and noted the white swan gracefully floating at the far side. He saw the gathering of people and wondered where this clan was located.

He tried to see what was happening, but the eagle kept its vision on the claw of an eagle that was on the edge of a circular hide.

Broken Spear fought to get the eagle to look at the people and then at the small figure that was put on the hide. He was unable to gain control. The eagle kept the claw in its vision.

Broken Spear watched as a small hand grasped the eagle's claw and raised it into the air.

His stomach seemed to go up into his throat as the eagle let out a joyous cry and took a spear like dive directly at the small figure holding up the claw.

He marveled at the focus the eagle kept on the claw and the precision that it exhibited as it grasped the claw and then rose into the sky.

The Ancients had proclaimed the holder of the claw as the person that would help the Bear Clan.

Broken Spear shared the vision and his experience with the Bear Clan Leadership. He cautioned that it would be a few seasons before that young hand that had held the claw would be old enough to be of any help. Until that time the clan leadership and the clan should take care of their own needs.

Broken Spear knew that his prediction would come to pass. He was just not sure when or how the events would occur.

And little did he know that it would be a young leader in one of the clans of the New Ones.

The End

About the Author

Ronald E. Mueller
remwriter95@gmail.com

Ron grew up in what is now Flint River State Park in Southeast Iowa. The 170-year-old house Ron lived in is built into a hillside. It faces a 125-foot-high cliff towering over the little Flint River. The house and the land talked to him about; the passing of time, the struggle to conquer the land, the struggles people faced and the wonder of nature.

He climbed the cliffs, crawled into the caves, dove from the swimming rock, collected clams from the bottom of the pond, gigged and skinned frogs for their legs. He trapped muskrats for fur, hunted raccoon in the dead of night, and with only a stick hunted rabbits in the dead of winter.

His young life was outdoors, and nature tested him.

He walked to a one room stone schoolhouse uphill both ways. A stern but warm-hearted teacher, Mrs. Henry was instrumental in shaping his character as she shepherded him from the fourth to the eighth grade.

It was a great way to grow up.

Ron graduated from Burlington, High School, went to Vietnam in the Navy. He graduated from The University of South Florida with a master's degree in engineering, worked for thirty eight years for Procter and Gamble, traveled around the world thirty times.

He has remained happily married for more than fifty years. His daughter and his two sons are all successful and his three grandchildren have all graduated.

His wife has humored and supported him as he became a full time professional story teller.

He has come to realize that he is, what is known as, a Cozy writer. Excitement and adventure but little guts and gore. His heroine or hero suffer a little but live happily ever after.

His experiences inter-twined with snippets of fantasy lend themselves to the adventures he leads the reader through.

Books by the Author

Fiction Series
The Taelo Series
The Early Years
The Golden Feather
Journey of Discovery
Dangerous Passage
Condor Clan Slingers
Circumvention
The Journey of Sages
Future Leaders Journey
Taelo Collection

A Taelo Story
White Swan and Quiet Pheasant
The Child's Name
Floating Cloud
Quiet Rabbit
Busy Bee
Little Otter & Talking Wren
Broken Spear
Burley Bear & Meadow Flower
Taelo Story Collection

The Alex Evercrest Series
The River Front
The Girl on The Grill
Missing
Maggot
Racist
Votive Candles
Windy City
Country Road
Pool of Blood
Sins of the Daughter
Body Parts
The Skull Collector
The Vanishing
The Shadow Fighter
Moonshine
Grief's Trajectory
The Magic Touch
Northern Lights
Alex Evercrest Heroine
Alex Evercrest Collection Two
New Direction
A Family Affair
Disruption
The St. Lebuinnus Church Murder

A Brian O'Neil Novel
Hawaiian Phoenix
Moon Curser
Death Broker

The Problem Solver Series
Solutions
Drug Lords
Border Crosser

The Problem Solver Collection
Science Fiction
The Savitar Series:
Journey's End
Savitar
Confluence
Savitar Series Collection

Bram Nielson Series
The Fold
The Message
Fold Wormhole
Negative Fold
Ripples in Time
Bram Nielson Collection

Single Science Fiction Books:
Current Past and Future
The Event
The Door
Viajante 7

https://www.remwriter95.net/

Around the world Publishing, LLC

9 781682 234037